To my friend Arjen
From David June 19, 1989

CRY
WILD

CRY WILD

R·D· LAWRENCE

SOUVENIR PRESS

PREFACE

Many years ago, when I heard my first wolf howl, I shivered with apprehension and clutched more tightly the gun that I was carrying, imagining that I was the reason for the wolf pack's song. Rational thinking was banished by the myths with which civilized man has been indoctrinated since pre-medieval times.

Nursery stories and blood-chilling folk tales passed in quick succession through my mind: the ghost of the Norse wolf, Fenris, giant and lustful for my flesh; the spectral werewolf, its bloodied, half-human mouth seeking my throat; the make-believe wolves from my childhood, which sought to feed exclusively on human flesh.

I stood in that spruce forest and the wolves howled around me and fear gripped me for several minutes. At last, ashamed of my superstitious emotions, I resumed my journey, but still apprehensive, my scalp tingling as the long, deep wails continued to pursue me.

It was not until I reached my Northern Ontario home that I relaxed. Then I became angry at myself. I had allowed ignorance to influence my emotions, and I determined that evening to learn the true ways of the wolf.

Now I bless the pack that gave me that imaginary scare. Because of it I have found peace and contentment and a deeper understanding. Above all I have become aware of the fullness of life, all life, and of the need to conserve it.

On that yesterday in the forest when the wolves howled I was a man ignorant of myself. I paid little heed to the true needs of life; I did not understand the subtly-strong bonds that exist between man and his natural environment.

Today I am aware that man must, if he is to survive, learn to tolerate the many other life forms that share his habitat. And if he is to tolerate them, he must understand them and he must also understand himself and the part that he plays within the circle of life.

Because of those howling wolves I learned that man must conserve his natural world or die with it.

ABOUT THIS BOOK

Cry Wild is partly fiction and mostly fact. The character of Morgan, the trapper, is purely imaginary; the plot relating to man and wolf is also fictional. But the details about the wolves and their way of life are, to the best of my knowledge, accurate. The facts are not as complete as I would like to have made them. This is because man does not yet know enough about the ways of the wolf. What we do know, however, proclaims clearly that the wolf is more sinned against than sinner.

This book is dedicated
to the Canadian wilderness
and to all those who care
about its preservation.

CRY
WILD

1

Grayness enveloped the land. Writhing clouds, leaden and tortured by swellings of moisture, hovered threatening over the evergreen forest. On winter-sered earth a covering of hard snow shone dull white, like the bloodless face of death, creating a mood of chill foreboding that matched the frowning sky.

It was afternoon. The gloom was a heavy thing that shrouded spruce and balsam, opaquing their green and forming dense, shapeless shadows within the private places of their branch coverings. No bird trilled gladness on this day. No squirrel called. Instead there was silence, and gloom, and cold, and the white threat of snow clouds waiting for their time to burst.

On a table-flat of land grew a mature balsam, a veteran tree; a tree of thick girth and spreading, brittle limbs; a mighty tree that had shaded its plot of earth with giant bulk and deprived other green life of its right to grow there. Within the conical spread of the balsam's lower limbs was a cavern of space, a circular natural tent that surrounded the leathery trunk.

, Curled in fitful slumber inside this matted shelter a bitch wolf lay. She was thin, this huntress of the forest, and aging, and her gray hair was matted and in places rubbed down to short bristles, exposing patches of scaly dark skin. She lay nose to tail. Her meagre flanks rose and fell slowly, in time with her lethargic breathing. Now and again a grunting whimper escaped through her black nostrils, for she was dreaming of the hunt and of sleek, lazy days when meat was plentiful and her belly round.

The bitch wolf had not eaten for three days, and four previous days of famine had conspired to shrivel her bowels and sap the coil-spring energy that motivated her lithe body.

Her meal three days ago had not been much: a portion of hare, thin and meagre, which she had stolen from a spitting bobcat. The bitch had smelled the kill and the killer while she was yet half a mile away from them. At any other time she would have changed course, leaving the cat to enjoy its spoils, but this was famine time in the forest, and her gnawing vitals had driven her towards the cat.

In a small cleared space that was ringed by spruce trees the tom cat was crunching fresh meat. It was noon and late for a kill, but hunger drove the hunters away from instinctive habits, and both the cat and the wolf were forced to seek meat.

The bitch wolf paused on the edge of the clearing, left forefoot up, arrested in the act of setting pad to snow crust. Her broad head with its long, sensitive muzzle was held high; the black nose, dull and dry and cracked, siphoned the aroma of hare newly dead, and the musky odour of angry cat. The wolf's black-lined lips curled upwards and downwards and the long, gleaming canines that flanked the white chisels of her cutting teeth were presented to the bobcat. A savage noise leaped from her throat.

The cat stopped eating. The bulge of a hastily gulped mouthful rippled down his short throat, and his answering growl, short and piercing, attempted to drive the wolf away. But the bitch needed the remains of the hare and she advanced, teeth bared and mouth agape, eyes fixed upon the cat. She was to eat this day. The leavings of the smaller hunter would be hers by right of conquest, and if the cat showed fight a great meal would be the prize, for the cat himself would die and become food for the starving wolf.

Instinct warned the bitch to avoid the chunky carnivore that stood, back arched and mouth ready, just paces away. But hunger drove her onward, the pain in her empty vitals signalling great need, a need that must be filled even at the cost of the hurt which must come from the claws and teeth of the cat. The bitch moved closer and snarled more loudly.

The arch formed by the spine of the bobcat became more pronounced. The round head dropped closer to the ground; short, tufted ears flattened against the skull. Now the right foreleg was raised, and the big paw was cupped and the claws showed black beneath the fur and the flesh of the pads. Closer came the bitch.

The cat's growls increased in pitch and tempo and a hissing, spitting sound came from the opened mouth. The yellow eyes were slitted, and there was great fury in the gaze that was glued upon the wolf. Closer yet came the bitch.

Now the cat moved. Holding his hump-backed pose he backed away from the hare, walking on stiff legs, moving with great slowness and much caution, wailing his banshee rage, but giving ground to an enemy made relentless by her empty belly. Closer came the bitch.

The cat broke. A last, ear-splitting wail of frustrated fury erupted from his open mouth. The yowl, incarnate with frenzy, seemed to hang over the clearing even after the bounding form of the snub-tailed cat disappeared into the underbrush.

The bitch gazed an instant at the place where the cat had vanished, then she turned to the hare's remaining flesh and the slaver fell from her mouth as she reached her muzzle for the food. Bones and meat and fur were crunched between the strong teeth and hastily swallowed, and the last remains of the snowshoe hare soon vanished. The portion had been small, the meal hasty, the time of its consumption but minutes on a human clock, but spartan as this feeding had been, life began to course anew through her depleted body.

She left the clearing. Only a few strands of white fur, some smudged stains of blood and the rumpled surface of snow marked the place where the duel for life had been won and lost. On leather-hard pads the she-wolf trotted through the forest, weak still, thin still, her famine showing in every movement. But the meal now inside her promised yet one more respite from death; slight, it is true, but hopeful.

Came three more days of hunger. In her white world the bitch searched without finding, while her last stores of strength left her. Her flanks pressed upwards towards her spine and her hip bones protruded sharply. She loped slowly, stopping at every hare form and brush pile, lifting her muzzle to search with nose and eyes among the branches of the evergreens, seeking signs of grouse. But there seemed to be no life in the wilderness and at last she sought shelter under the great balsam fir and curled her miseries around herself and slept. And dreamed of sleek days.

This was December, a lean wicked month made waspish by the stab of frosts that nightly drove temperatures down to forty degrees below zero. The bitch had met this kind of month before, and she had met, too, the months that preceded it, when the autumn gave warning of the Great Cold: when scarlet leaves were plucked early from their branchlets; when the birds pointed south and the berries withered on their stalks; and when the snow hare changed his coat from brown to white four weeks before his time, then seemed to disappear off the face of the frozen earth. And the bitch wolf knew that when the snow hare goes, the time of famine is near, for the big hare with the great feet is life to the hunters of the forest.

So, before the famine, the bitch had led her pack towards the south, away from the knifing of cold and the smothering whiteness that made travel hard for even those such as she, sinuous, powerful huntress though she was. And her pack followed, content, as usual, to let her show the way. Had she not always led well and found meat when none was to be had? Last autumn seven wolves made up the pack: the bitch and her mate, a big, rawboned dog two years younger than she; a two-year-old male, not yet ready to mate, who had somehow become unattached and had joined the pack rather than wander alone through the forest; and the four pups that had been born to her last May and were now half grown. This was the she's pack, and she led them that autumn away from the killing frosts and south, to a domain she had never before visited. And this was her mistake.

They broke out of the forest early one morning in late November and saw before them a land still green, a new kind of land of slopes and valleys and few trees and much grass. And grazing upon the grass was a new kind of animal.

The bitch was unsure at first. She stopped and tested the wind, and the odour of the creatures in the clearing came strong to her senses. This new smell was almost acrid in its intensity. It assailed the she's sensitive nostrils, like and yet different to the scent of the deer she and her pack had so often hunted. Instinct told her that the slow-moving things before her would furnish the pack with food. Her alert senses told her that these animals would be easy to kill. These were stupid creatures, or why did they continue to pull at the grass in the presence of the pack? There was no sign of alarm amongst the flock of sheep, and even more noticeable to the wolf was the absence of a leader. No nervous, restless buck was there to stop his grazing and look up and around, big ears testing for signs of danger. The bitch wolf wondered why, and something within her cried a warning that made her whine indecision.

Not so her mate. The big dog looked at the she, his manner urging her to rise from her haunches and lead the pack in the hunt, but when she remained sitting, undecided, he waited no more. Only some seventy yards separated the wolves from their quarry, and the dog was not disposed to caution. An excited yelp left his throat as he flung his body into a fast lope.

The others followed him; all except the bitch. She stayed where she was, watching the pack converge on the flock, which even then showed no alarm. The old male wolf was the first to strike. A ewe lifted her head to stare at him and now there was panic in the sheep eyes. But too late did she bleat fear and begin to bunch her slender legs for the run. The wolf was onto her, charging her with his shoulder, knocking her down with his massive weight, and before the sheep's kicking legs moved twice through the air his fangs sank into her throat and the life was torn from her.

The sight of the kill and the smell of the blood drove the wolves to frenzy. They killed and killed again, slaying easily and quickly, running down the crazed creatures who were too stupid to escape and whose puny legs could not hope to outdistance the great lithe creatures who pursued them. Nine sheep now lay bleeding on the frosted grass and the rest of the flock was scattered over the meadow, their bleats of panic creating bedlam in the stillness.

The wolves settled to their feast, but still the bitch sat on the edge of the clearing, her gaze fixed upon the carnage ahead. Hunger urged her to go and eat, yet that inborn caution she had felt as soon as she saw the strange, docile creatures held her anchored. She sat as her pack had left her, mouth open, white teeth agleam, the redness of her lolling tongue a flash of colour against her grizzled coat. She quivered. Her body shook as though with ague, and eagerness seized her, an almost irresistible urge, driving her towards the meat that lay waiting upon the grass. And another emotion gripped her and fought with her eagerness and she shook the more, for this thing deep inside her was stronger than her desire for food. This was fear, stark and vivid and primordial. And it held her back.

She was still there when the men came and the guns exploded and her pack rolled in agony beside the mutilated sheep. All except the two-year-old wolf. He ran, dodging the bullets and the men who raced after him in a roaring, rattling machine, and he led the men away from the bitch wolf.

She slunk back into the forest and once more turned her muzzle towards the north woods, in her ears the still-rowdy clamour of the men and their machine. The bitch galloped now, setting her long legs to a fast pace and attaining a speed of some twenty-five miles an hour. She ran thus for more than an hour, then she slowed to the mile-consuming lope that she could maintain for many hours at a time. Straight north she ran, oblivious of her surroundings or of the creatures she passed. Twice a white-tailed deer fled from her path unnoticed, and once a silver fox sprang up almost from under her pads; yet, despite her hunger, she did not pause to strike and kill, but ran on, concerned only with finding the sanctuary of the deep woods, away from the haunts of men.

When the bitch wolf at last stopped the sun was seeking the underside of the earth. It was not yet dark, but long shadows filled the bushland, and the bedding-sound of winter's birds was becoming stilled. Where the wolf now stood, flanks heaving with urgent breath, mouth agape and dripping heat moisture, was heavy forest land, wild and tangled, clustered with jack pine and tamarack and birch, cloaked with bush growth and dead ferns and sered grass. Instinct had brought her here, and now she sought a hidden place in which to sleep and restore herself after the great run of that day. A downed pine, interlaced with choking creeper and brush, offered her shelter and concealment, and she crawled under, circling three times in her chosen bed-ground in the age-old ritual of the dog seeking to smooth with broad pads the place where sleep will come.

In the face of torpid slumber the biting in her empty vitals fled. Snow came that night, a light sprinkling of white that coated the forest, but she slept unaware until the coming of a sickly dawn.

The bitch wolf woke and stood, shaking the snow from her body and stretching the stiffness from her muscles. She smelled the morning, back humped, head held high as her nostrils sucked in the effluvia of the forest: the scent of cold, the faint odour of decay coming through the snow from the forest floor; the aroma of the pines; the vague fetor of animal life. Suddenly, there was the strong smell of grouse, a subtle, hunger-reviving odour that brought drool into the wolf mouth and instantly alerted the hunting senses.

The stretched muscles were allowed to return to normal, and the legs found their customary stance. The bitch stood tall and still and silent, sniffing; smelling out the one odour, separating it from all the rest, probing for its source. She had it now. It came from the northeast, and in her hunter's brain, computations were made that told her many things. There was distance yet between her and the grouse; and there were several birds, three perhaps, judging by the subtle differences in each aroma. Satisfied that she had allowed her nose time enough to discover all, the bitch set out, letting her nostrils be her guide, stepping softly and with care, seeking the cover of pine and brush; slowly advancing towards her quarry, noting with each step the increased flavour of the smell that now linked her invisibly, like some fine guide-line, to her quarry.

There was infinite patience in her silent hunt that morning; great care, and untold ages of hunting guile bequeathed by her sires. Her need was pressing, her hunger great, but instinct and experience warned that haste could only result in more hunger.

The scent-trail led through heavy forest, up a slight incline, and down into a shallow valley. Here the odour was strong. The wolf stopped; her nose probed, discovering that there were now four smells, each proclaiming grouse, yet each slightly different from the others, which told her that there were four birds sheltering in the valley.

The wolf crouched low. She set out again, almost bellying her way down the slope, keeping her dark body hidden behind whatever cover she could find, now and then pausing to reassure herself that the breeze was still blowing towards her, from the direction of her quarry. Ten more minutes of human time ticked by, and then the bitch wolf knew that she must stop and find her quarry with her eyes. The smell now was so strong that one of the birds must be within leaping distance. She flattened herself on the ground, her body blended with the forest floor, her immobility almost lifeless; her eyes searched minutely, with painstaking, inching purpose, scanning every twig, every mound of snow, every shadow and log. Thus she discovered the grouse.

It was a cock bird, brown and sturdy and plump, and it sat resting in the lee of a young pine. Its head faced away from the wolf, for it was engrossed in the antics of three hens which, out of sight of the wolf, were scratching with sturdy, hairy feet at the snow, seeking frost-nipped cranberries that had fallen from a high bush that stood nearby. The bitch became a statue. Her yellow eyes were full of the killer urge, her lips drawn back, exposing white teeth in a snarl that remained silent in her throat. She inched forward, first stretching her body to its full, then moving slowly, silently, until the powerful springing muscles were coiled, the feet and legs braced and quivering beneath bunched haunches.

The wolf's stalk was soundless, yet something, perhaps the deeply-rooted instinct of self-preservation, alerted the cock grouse. He sat higher and his neck leaned, so that now his head was raised several inches higher. From his partly-opened beak a soft but penetrating whistle escaped. The hens stopped scratching and took up the warning sound and began pacing in undecided manner, their necks held forward, low to the ground, their stubby tails stiff on a horizontal plane, their crests erect. The cock rose from his place of rest and imitated his mates, but none of the birds was yet sure where the danger lurked. Still peeping, hoping that their call and their movement would cause the danger to reveal itself, they high-stepped through the underbrush, and all the birds were revealed to the waiting bitch. She could restrain herself no longer. As she leaped for the cock bird, the grouse burst into noisy action. Into all directions they exploded, their stubby wings beating a drum-roll as they rose from the ground.

The bitch wolf touched ground with her front paws, followed through with her back legs and launched herself again, this time rearing upwards and leaping mightily, her mouth reaching for the swiftly-winging shape of the cock bird. For an instant the wilderness scene became as though frozen. There hung the bitch, hind legs fully extended, their mighty sinews showing through the hair and flesh like tensile steel ropes, and above them the sculpted, lean belly and flanks, the deep chest, and the front legs with their great paws held below the taut neck that narrowed slightly where the spine enters the brain and then broadened into the wide head that in its turn fined down to the muzzle and the shining black nose. And beneath the pointed muzzle were the fangs, the hunting fangs of the wolf that were even then about to close upon the feathered breast of the grouse. The brief illusion ceased. Action returned to the scene; the flashing teeth found flesh and closed upon it, and the lean body was pulled back to earth again, leaving nothing in the airspace so recently occupied by the bird.

As the wolf's feet touched the snow anew, a burst of brown and gray feathers rose upwards, spread and drifted away. The grouse hung limp in the wolf's jaws, dead. The bitch stumbled slightly, regained her balance, and stood still for an instant, her nose and taste glands savouring the body of her prey. She lowered her head and relaxed her great jaws, and the bird dropped inert upon the rumpled snow. Three bright drops of crimson leaked from under the feathers and melted a place upon the white ground. The bitch licked her bloody lips, then settled to her kill.

Afterwards she slept. It was a short sleep, light, the vigilant doze of a beast that has fed; a sleep finely atuned to the movements of the forest, satisfying the demands of a busy digestion yet meeting the dictates of inborn caution. It was a needed sleep, for the bitch was not yet fully rested after the panic that was now gone, but which still pestered the brain into torpid feelings of fear that were more fatiguing than physical exertion.

For one hour by the clocks of man the bitch slept while life melted from the forest that housed her, for the smell of death clung to the wolf. The beasts and birds sought sanctuary elsewhere; they sensed that the wolf, now a sleeping effigy made harmless and dull by slumber, would soon awake and hunt again, for one grouse, though plump, is not enough to fully sate the hunger of an active wolf.

And while the creatures of the forest stole away on silent pads and wings, the bitch, restless, dreamed. The jumbled vagaries of fact-fancy awoke the bitch wolf. And she raised herself and pointed to the sky and her cavernous mouth opened and her long, tremulous howl floated free to lose itself in space and time and to mingle with the laments of countless other wolves now dead. The despair in her voice lived. It forced itself from her lungs and up the channel of her throat and was given shape and substance by the mouth and tongue. Then it sailed death-less away, leaving the she-wolf spent and head-fallen, her mouth hanging loose, a small bead of moisture slowly easing its way down her red tongue towards the frozen ground.

In the wolf's mind was the remembrance of yesterday, of the terror of man, an ageless ancient thing that reigned supreme among the fears which eons of evolution had embedded in the nature of the beast. There was remembrance, also, of her pack, and there was loneliness, and this loosed a whine of eagerness from the bitch. She needed those of her own kind around her and her loneliness drove her, urging her to seek those which, to her, still existed — her cubs, her mate, and the young dog-wolf, dead things all by the standards of man, deathless in the wolf mind, which would seek until it found solace in new company.

The wolf raised her head. Her tongue flicked quickly over her chops. A disappointingly-faint savour of grouse rewarded the action, serving only to whet the appetite, reminding the bitch of her need. She rose to all fours and stretched her body, scent-ing the forest for prey which had fled, knowing that this would be so, yet ever hopeful that some creature, old or sick, had remained to furnish her with a new meal. But there was nothing; and so the she-wolf moved from her bedding ground and geared her legs to the slow lope, the hunting pace fast enough to carry her away from this now empty forest, but slow enough to allow her nose and her ears and her eyes time to search for prey. And as she ran the shrunken belly pressed upwards towards the spine and the once regal brush found sanctuary between her haunches and was pushed upwards, to hug the lean, taut gut. Four days later she stole the hare from the bobcat.

For three more days, the bitch loped through the forest, pressing ever north and west, seeking the dense wilderness; and during this time not once did she see or hear or smell another living creature. Now she stopped. A cursory glance at her surroundings was enough to tell her that she was still alone, and she whined a little before she allowed her head to hang, mouth agape, while her laboured lungs pumped and pumped again, replenishing with oxygen the over-worked blood supplies.

It was early afternoon and there hung over the wilderness the certainty of snow. Past the tallest trees drifted heavy black clouds and there was a feel in the air presaging the violence of winter. The storm was imminent and the bitch knew it, and she sought a place of shelter, ignoring her hunger and her weakness with the stoicism of her kind. But there was scant shelter here and she pushed her body into motion again, this time pumping faster with her legs as she fled through the forest on her new quest. She ran thus for another half-hour and then she stopped anew, for her quick eyes had spotted the awaiting shelter of the tall balsam.

Within this matted sanctuary she smoothed her bed and curled her body and closed her eyes in sleep. And the wind came and the hovering clouds burst and the flakes of white fell upon the wilderness and shrouded the wolf in her bower.

All afternoon the snow fell. Inch by inch it piled higher upon the land, drifting in open places, packing into the brush and into the branches of the trees. Only the howl of the wind could be heard, for even the movement of the tree branches went unnoticed before the storm's wrath. And then, suddenly, the wind stilled. Now there was silence, the intense, cold silence of a storm-freed northern wilderness.

The clouds were spent. They trundled about the sky aimlessly, pushed along by the high winds that blew not on earth; and as they slipped away, strong light began to reach the bushland and the tree-tops became tinted with the red of the setting sun. They are strange, these abrupt changes of a northland winter. Now the world is a shrieking, savage place; now it is a silent, green-and-white canvas agleam with beauty. But the silence and the colour and the beauty are deceptive things. This is still the same wilderness; it is still savage, and still dangerous.

Under the balsam, the she-wolf slept. The red of the sun faded and was gradually replaced by the blue of twilight, which in turn ran before the advancing dark. The forest was a ghostly place of outlines, two-toned in the gray-whiteness of night snow and the opaque bulk of trees and brush that blended into vague, gargantuan shapes. An hour passed; two. Stars shone, each a-sparkle with the shine of living fire. A broad swath of green luminescence blazed a trail across the black sky. Creation stared down from the strange, unknown immensity.

The sleeping wolf twitched to wakefulness and shrugged the covering of snow from her body. She rose and stretched; then she sat on her haunches, remaining within the shelter of her tree, ears upright, nostrils testing for scent, eyes scanning the forest. She shook herself to free the last particles of snow from her coat, and stepped away from the balsam. The snow reached to her chest, so that she had to bound in order to travel through it, and in her state of weakness this called for almost more strength than she could muster. But life is stubborn in the wilderness and the bitch wolf refused to die. On she went, a slow, laboured progress that carried her southwards. Often she stopped for breath, and often she paused to scan the forest and to listen to it in the hope of discovering prey.

In this manner the night became spent and a paleness arose in the sky. The snow became harder, for the forest was more open, and it furnished footing for the big feet of the wolf. But it was treacherous footing. Now and then she would break through the snow crust and great effort was required to scramble out of the depth and regain the crust. When she climbed up on it she would sit and rest, head held low, mouth open, her thin flanks pulsing in and out with the fast rhythm of her gasping breath. Death came a little closer to the she-wolf that morning.

Then she smelled food, and at once she changed. The listless eyes glinted: the chest-hugging tail eased itself out from between the legs. She was a huntress again. The creature was a porcupine; the wolf knew this by its smell. At another time she would have passed by this bristly beast, for there is danger in the slow, docile porcupine. But today she had no choice; she must face those deadly-sharp quills if she was to live.

The porcupine was only yards in front of the wolf. It was vainly trying to reach the sanctuary of a tall balsam, caught in the open between its den and a tree. The wolf hurried, her snarl low but clear, a deliberate sound uttered to intimidate the quill-pig. The porcupine heard and stopped its struggle with the snow, and this was the design of the wolf's growl. Now the porcupine would remain at bay: it knew that it could not outdistance that growl, that its only hope of survival lay in the sharp defences that it could muster.

The wolf slowed, perhaps not anxious to begin the attack on this bristly enemy, perhaps aware that there was no hurry now, for the porcupine would not turn, could not run.

The porcupine was a hunched black figure atop the hardpacked snow. Its long winter hair trapped light-rays and reflected them again and its ebon shone with a mixture of colour. Plentiful among the black hairs were the quills, pale yellow, with needle tips pointed black, and each one of them was now erect. The stubby tail, where the heavier quills were, was already sweeping back and forth across the surface of the snow; the small round head was buried between the stiff forelegs: the shoe-button eyes were alert, able, despite the protecting legs, to watch the enemy's advance.

Now the wolf was within feet of the porcupine. She tried to outflank her prey, and at once the porcupine swivelled on its front legs, keeping its menacing tail before the wolf. Again the bitch turned, moving in; again the porcupine swivelled and the wolf backed off. The two settled to their deadly battle: the wolf hungry, made desperate by her need, the hump-backed porcupine aware that death would follow one slow movement, one slight miscalculation.

Suddenly the bitch wolf turned away. Had she abandoned the fight? She took two strides away from her victim: then, summoning from her almost depleted reserves a flash of speed, she turned again to the attack. But her ruse failed. Again she was faced by the slashing, quill-forested tail, and she retreated.

The battle continued. The two were like trained duellists, feinting, dodging, the wolf seeking to reach the porcupine's defenceless head, the porcupine intent always on presenting its formidable tail to the enemy. If the wolf should once be able to grasp the round, quill-free nose, the porcupine would die; if the porcupine could but smash its bristling tail into the wolf's face, the wolf would most likely die and the porcupine would escape. The prize for each combatant was life.

One hour passed. The wolf was tiring, and her elusive quarry seemed as fresh as ever. Try as she would, she could not get in front of the porcupine which, using its stiff front legs as an axis, pivoted easily and swiftly to meet with its tail every lunge made by the wolf. Twice the armoured tail of the porcupine brushed the wolf's muzzle and she retreated to wipe at the soreness with a broad front paw; the quills were not firmly embedded and they came away, leaving minute droplets of crimson and a sting of fire. It seemed that the fight had reached an impasse, but the weakened wolf would not give up. Instead she redoubled her charges, increased her speed; and now the porcupine's actions were not as sure, its turns not as swift.

Suddenly the bitch leaped at her quarry, her growl loud, savage. Right over the crouching porcupine she went, but instead of hurtling into the deep snow she twisted her lean body in mid-air and landed with her flashing jaws just inches from the coveted place; in another instant the jaws moved and she had secured a good grip on the porcupine's head. Now she started moving backwards, dragging the wildly thrashing porcupine, the while tightening her grip on the head. The porcupine fought. It pulled back and tried to reach the wolf with its flailing tail, but it was weakening, the blood was flowing, and the wolf kept pulling back, back. . . . There was no hope now for the porcupine; it would die this day, and the bitch wolf would live. At last it was over. The powerful jaws of the wolf, her long, sharp canine teeth, did their work; and the porcupine died.

The wolf relaxed her hold and moved back a step. She licked her lips and savoured the blood of her victim, then she examined her right forefoot, which showed the ivory yellow of three quills firmly embedded between two toes. The wolf licked the burning place, carefully, then she pulled back her lips and with an air of daintiness lowered her gleaming teeth to her paw and pulled out the quills one at a time, gripping each firmly with her cutting teeth. When this was done, she licked her paw, spending some time on it, seeming to enjoy the taste of her own blood.

The wolf rose and turned to the dead porcupine. Carefully she reached out a paw, hesitated, then put it down again. She stood over the carcass, front legs spread, head hanging so that her nose was almost touching the porcupine. Then she gripped the mangled head and lifted the carcass clear of the ground. She swung her head so that the dead creature flew grotesquely in the air and its descending body threatened to fall on top of her. But she sidestepped and let her grip go at the same time and the porcupine fell to the snow on its back, the soft, unprotected belly exposed to the wolf's teeth. The bitch lowered her head and bit into her prey. She ate, slowly, savouring each mouthful, eating her victim from the inside, taking care that the carcass stayed on its back so that most of the quills remained harmlessly buried in the snow. Some quills found their way into her mouth, but these were crushed between the molars. If their points would later embed themselves in the lining of her stomach and intestines, they would not cause her death, for, somehow, such quills are robbed of their power by the gastric juices of the wolf.

Half an hour later the wolf was finished. Some fifteen pounds of fresh meat and bone filled her shrivelled belly, and the time of want, the spectre of death, the cold, the tired, aching body, were but vague, bad memories. She licked herself clean, spent a little more time on her hurt paw, and then sought a place to sleep. Tonight she would travel again, refreshed, strong.

2

There was stillness, and moonlight, and a thousand shadows and as many reflections, for the forest in this place was broken by the oblong of a wilderness lake. And there was snow, much snow. It sparkled where it met the moonlight and it lay dead and white in the shadows of the trees. But it was on the lake that the snow really lived, for here it was packed hard, burnished by the wind, which had compressed it onto the layer of heavy ice that upheld its weight: here the snow was like a scattering of sequins, shining blue and green and red and silver.

It was February, a bitter month to some creatures of the northland, a time of snow crusts that break beneath sharp hoofs and cut them with their knife-edges so that the blood comes; a time of cold, great cold, and of hunger, and of death. A lonely time for some, a fearful time, yet also a time of life, for there are many forest things that breed during this month.

It was such a month for the bitch wolf. She sat this night upon an outcrop of granite, her haunches spread over the snow, her front legs stiff, her back and shoulders at an angle to the moon, her fine eyes fixed upon the snow-bound lake. Now and then she whined, for she was made restless by the mating urge, and she was lonely, and she had not yet met a questing dog. She listened to the night; but it held no invitation to her and she whined again. Tonight she was full and she was strong and her time of want was long passed; but she was unhappy, for wolves are sociable creatures and she had been alone all winter and now, when all her being cried for a mate, she sat on that outcrop of granite staring at an empty forest. The bitch wolf whined again, then she raised her broad head so that her sharp muzzle pointed directly at the sky. She pushed her ears back, holding them against her head, and she opened her great mouth and she cried her anguish at the night. Her call was deep and throaty, a clear sound, long and low, yet it carried far into the night: *a—woo . . . a—woo . . . a—woo . . . woooooo.* And when she was finished she hung her head and raised her ears, flicking them from side to side.

For perhaps one minute there was silence, then an answer reached her. It was faint, for it had travelled across more than a mile of forest, yet it reached her. She raised her head and pointed to the sky again and she launched her call anew. More silence, again an answer, and this time it was just a little stronger. The bitch howled once more; back came a reply. And now she rose, stretched, and bounded into the forest, heading towards the west to intercept the male who had answered her call. The dog would, she knew, be trotting as she was, running east to meet her.

Both animals were silent now. Each had located the other; there was no more need for the howling call to guide. Instinct drove them unerringly towards their trysting place.

The bitch wolf smiled as she ran. Her eyes softened, her lips were parted wide, revealing her gleaming teeth and the pink cavity of her mouth. There was no trace of savagery in the gaping jaws, just a show of friendship, a light of eagerness in the eyes. This was the wolf smile, a physical sign as clearly denoting pleasure and happiness as the widest of human grins. She ran on, seemingly oblivious of all, yet vibrantly alive to the sights and sounds of the forest. She noticed three grouse cowering under a balsam fir; the fresh scent of running deer penetrated her nostrils; a hare streaked for cover and was unconsciously followed by her yellow eyes. Still she ran, mentally cataloguing these signs of food.

Now and then one of her paws would break through the snow crust and she would stumble, recover, then continue on her journey. Once, as she was passing a rotting stump, she paused and allowed her nostrils to brush over it. This was a scent station, one of the many special places used by wolves to record their passage through the forest. A male had stopped here several hours earlier to urinate, the chemistry of his desires mixed with his waste. And beneath this latest odour were others. Two she-wolves had passed this way, and three other males, and the scent of each told its own story to the bitch wolf. The two she-wolves had come and gone days before, closely followed by the three males; these scents were of no interest now. But the fresh odour of a dog wolf on the prowl for a mate aroused the bitch further. She squatted and added her scent to the stump, turned and briefly sniffed at the combined odours, then resumed her journey.

The forest through which she ran was a place of almost pure darkness. Countless spruce trees jostled for growing room and conspired to shut out the moonlight. Beneath the snow, their roots were knotted and turned in layer after layer of sphagnum moss which was frozen into a solid mass now, but which would be soft and wetly treacherous during the spring and summer. In this place only the spruce trees grew; and the forest floor, beneath the snow, was thickly carpeted by brown, dead needles that the trees had shed. During the growing seasons a few stunted blueberry bushes managed to cling to precarious life. In this place the white-tailed deer found shelter from the storms of winter; and here, too, the wolves sought the deer, while ruffed grouse and spruce grouse clucked and peeped as they slithered atop the snow or flew in explosive bursts from tree to tree, their quick wings and fanned tails carrying them along an erratic, dodging course among the tightly-packed tree trunks.

Red squirrels lived in the trees, their bulky woven nests anchored securely to sturdy branches twenty or thirty feet from the ground. Sharing their tall world the gray jays called often with their many voices of mimicry, and sought to steal the seeds that the squirrels husbanded. In this place skulked the lynx; great, lithe cats ever seeking the grouse and the squirrels and the few snowshoe hares that also made this their sanctuary. Here the bitch wolf met her mate.

He was a young male seeking to breed this season for the first time, and he was eager. He ran with careless abandon, endowed with the enthusiasm of youth, a virile young savage whose great size and strength made him confident of himself. There was a touch of arrogance in his being. He was brash and had much yet to learn. And he was beautiful. His sleek heavy coat was a charcoal black, and lightly laced with gray. He stood three feet at the shoulders, and the power of him was quickly evident in the sure movements of his sturdy legs and in the broad, heavily-boned proportions of his head. Intellect was reflected in the eyes that were now made brighter by the lust that gripped him. He ran grinning, his ears pricked forward, his neck outstretched, his handsome tail trailing like a black plume, its tip pointing towards the snow.

The bitch and the dog heard each other's movements while still separated by a quarter of a mile of forest. Each paused a moment and their ears inched forward still further; then they ran with greater swiftness. Minutes later they saw each other. Both creatures stopped. Wariness and gladness showed in their gaze. The dog whined and advanced a few steps, stopped and whined again, his head held to one side, his nostrils busy with the new scent, the wolf smile prominent in his eyes and on his lips. The bitch stood still. She held her head high, her ears flattened, the smile on her mouth tinged with warning. She wanted time to inspect this youngster. The dog advanced a few more steps and when he stopped, he bowed, sliding his forelegs along the snow and depressing his chest, his head still held to one side and his eyes looking up at the bitch. His whine of excitement was higher, his body quivered with emotion. He bounded sideways suddenly, chased his tail for three revolutions, then bowed again as the bitch moved forward, stopped, and copied his antics. In this way they drew closer, in an ancient ritual of greeting, the wariness gone now from their eyes and replaced by open affection.

They stood shoulder to shoulder, still as statues. One moment, two, then the she-wolf moved. Swiftly she nipped the black dog's shoulder, rose on her hind legs, and leaped over him to go racing through the trees. The dog gave swift chase and the snow flew from their pads as they ran madly around the trees. As quickly as she moved, the bitch stopped and turned to face the oncoming dog. He stopped then, half a length away from her. Both bowed, the bitch to the right, the dog to the left, and the bitch nipped him again, but it was affection that powered the bite. The dog was made bolder and he rushed her. She retreated, still facing him, growling a little, but her every action a coy invitation. Again they stood side by side but facing in opposite directions, tails wagging rapidly. The dog lowered his head and scented the bitch. She halted the motion of her tail and she turned towards the dog, quiescent.

Then they mated, and the seeds of life took root within the bitch wolf. This was the ritual of creation, the act of union between two beings, as natural as the wilderness, as ancient as the beginning of time.

March replaced February, and there were nights of intense cold and high, screaming winds that burnished the deep snow and hardened its crust. The wilderness shuddered during those nights and its creatures sought shelter within the embrace of tangled spruce and balsam. There they lay quietly in their beds of snow, the solitary ones huddled in tight balls, the companionable ones seeking warmth from each other's bodies. If daybreak stilled the wind they arose and searched for food, but if the blizzard still raged they stayed in their shelters, hungry, preferring the gnaw of their bellies to the death-grip of the icy wind.

In a dense patch of balsams the bitch wolf and her mate had scooped a den within the shelter of a downed tree. Each was curled nose to tail, each slept, the pumping of their lungs barely disturbing the snow-covered outlines of their bodies. They slept, empty of belly but content. The signs spoke of a sun-filled day that was yet to come; then they would hunt, for this storm had lasted three days and there had been no food during that time. Hunting would be harder during daylight, but the two healthy wolves were unconcerned. The range upon which they had settled held abundant game, and the two, full of instinctive self-confidence, knew that they would satisfy their hunger with sunrise and a change in the weather.

New life was already stirring inside the bitch. Soft, jerking movements occasionally pulsed her sides as the unborn litter became restless. Imprisoned in the birth membranes of the bitch wolf there were four tiny mites, as yet not fully formed, but already seeming to be impatient to be born. And each time they wriggled their little sausage shapes the she-wolf felt them and was content, the hardships of this winter blotted out by her brief mating and the fretful comfort of the young inside her belly. Now she snored a little.

Around the two, the evergreens shook their needles as the wind buffeted them. Snow lanced through the darkness, and the wind moaned its hollow dirge as though crying that it would soon be banished from the land by the warmer breath of spring. There must always be one last night of winter, and this was it.

Already the wind was losing some of its power and there was more space between the flakes of snow; the trees trembled less, the loose snow drifted more freely. In the east a vague glow showed fleetingly above the tree-tops. Slowly, slowly, the wild wind from the north tired, blew less fiercely, and at last was still. Now nothing moved. The land was as a thing dead, a contoured map of white and dark in the intense stillness of pre-dawn.

The wolves stirred in unison. They uncurled, stiffly, breaking the caked layer of snow that cloaked their bodies. They rose and shook, and showers of white flew from them. The dog licked the bitch's muzzle; it was a caress, a love greeting. The bitch bowed to him and pranced a little, her eyes alive with excitement. Her mate whined and dove at her and the two flayed through the snow in play, grim hunters relaxed in the joy of living. As quickly as their game began it stopped and the two stood immobile for a fraction of time. Then the bitch walked slowly towards the south, leading her mate on the hunt. Gone now was the playfulness.

Before them the forest was a place of fading black, gripped by the quiet of this new day. The birds of the north were sleeping still, and the hares remained crouched in their forms. A snowy owl passed silently overhead, his great white body a moving blur against the deep shadows of the trees. There seemed to be no life remaining in the forest. But there was, and the wolves knew this.

The bitch continued to lead. Both animals moved with the long-legged, wolfish lope that appeared slow, yet covered the ground at a goodly speed. The bitch carried her head high, and her nostrils constantly tested the air. Her mate used his nose to probe the surface of the snow, to test the trees and bushes they were passing. For fifteen minutes they continued thus, treading easily on the surface of the snow, their big pads supporting them on the frozen crust.

Suddenly, the she-wolf stopped, and instantly her mate emulated her. Both wolves probed the air, their ears pricked. One moment, two, then the bitch changed course, turning to the east, towards the glow of the sun. She galloped, her mate following, the snow flying behind their kicking heels as they raced to intercept the scent that had alerted them.

Somewhere ahead of them, not far, there were deer; their scent proclaimed them. And as the wolves ran, their keen senses analyzed the problems of this hunt. There were at least three deer in this band. The quarry was moving but not fleeing in panic, and this was good, for it meant that the hunters were, so far, undetected. Soon the movement of the deer became clearly audible to the hunting wolves and, by the sudden quickening of it, the hunters knew that their own scent and the noise of their passage had alarmed their prey. The hunters ran faster, throwing their great bodies into the powerful, wearing gallop that could be sustained for hours, long after their fleeter quarry had been run down.

The chase led through thick forest. An army of scaly spruce trees stretched into infinity in this place where the sun seldom reached the earth. The signs in the snow told the wolves that this was the bedding place of the deer. Scooped beds, oval indentations in the snow at the foot of shaggy trees, showed where the creatures had slept out the storm. Droppings, small brown ovals still agleam with frozen moisture, were plentiful, and tiny yellow craters in the snow told of urine stops. The snow was deeply furrowed by the slim legs and sharp hoofs of the deer. Here and there the snow crust had cut into the deer's pasterns, and the odour of fresh blood excited the wolves further. They yelped to each other and lunged harder into their run.

The bitch turned her head and looked full at her mate. The dog understood her signal. He changed course, leaving her to run at the heels of the quarry while he pointed himself towards the northeast, redoubling his stride and quickly disappearing into the forest. The she-wolf barked. It was not the bark of a domestic dog, but a high-pitched yelping sound repeated often as she ran, its purpose clearly to put more panic into the fleeing deer.

The bitch gradually changed the direction of her travel, angling towards the southeast, turning the quarry, herding them towards her mate, who was by now almost ready to intercept the fleeing animals. The deer began to turn, to swing slightly to the north, unaware of the trap that had been laid for them. The bitch was aware that her manoeuvre was working and she yelped louder and ran faster, driving the deer harder, crowding more panic into their minds.

So the chase continued, the fleeing deer wearing down their

strength as they plunged through the deep snow crusts which would not support the knife-stabs of their black hoofs. The pursuing bitch was gaining steadily and was herding the quarry towards her waiting mate. The sun rose, and daylight aided the hunters. Now and then the bitch caught sight of a fleeing deer — a quickly-kicking hoof, a waving, white tail. Now, too, she could see the carmine of blood staining the snow of the trail, evidence that the ice crusts were taking their toll from those tender pasterns.

More than an hour had passed since the two wolves took up the hunt. For the last half of this time, the male had been sitting atop a small knoll, waiting for the quarry to come closer. He had followed his mate's progress attentively and he had known at once that she was succeeding in her intent. It was only a question of time, so he had composed himself, patiently waiting the moment of the kill. Presently he tensed with excitement and rose to all fours. The quarry was close, very close. He moved forward to intercept, husky, healthy, and fresh from his rest. The hunt was his now. His mate had put all her mighty strength into her bid to turn the herd towards where he stood, ready to bound into slashing action upon a quarry that was almost at the point of exhaustion.

The wolf and the deer sighted each other simultaneously. The wolf bunched his tough body for the final effort; the deer, three of them, turned away from him in frantic haste. The wolf was a flashing ball of black fury. One of the deer was slower than the rest. Yard by yard the wolf gained, encouraged by the excited yelps of his mate, who, though lagging, was still in the chase. The leading deer sped onward; the laggard stumbled once, righted herself and tried to gain on the bared fangs that were only yards away from her kicking legs. But relentlessly the wolf closed the gap and now he was running beside the deer, perhaps two feet from her. He called on his reserves, his flashing legs moved just a little faster, and he was up to the doe's shoulder. Suddenly he lunged into the fleeing deer. The impact of his weight against her front legs sent the doe crashing to the snow. In a flash the wolf was upon her. His questing fangs found the throat and tasted the warm fresh blood that gushed out and spread quickly over the snow. The deer died quickly, and by the time the bitch arrived, her mate was already feeding. She settled beside him and sank her gleaming teeth into the warm meat. The doe was old and barren; she was sick from the fly whose larvae eat into the nasal passages of deer; and these things had made her slow, and easy prey for the dog wolf.

The hunters fed, greedily. Fangs and cutting teeth tore at the deer; powerful muscles of shoulder and neck and chest tensed and pulled sharply; the gripping teeth wrenched meat from the carcass. The wolves fed silently, yet there was noise; small sounds, made by the ripping of flesh, by the quick chewing of meat, by the quick gulps as the meat was forced down almost whole. And then the meal was over. Almost twenty pounds of meat had been crammed into each belly. The wolves were distended when they sat upright and washed, cleaning the blood from their faces and chests.

The bitch yawned, a huge gape that ended in a sudden whine. The dog wagged his tail at her and watched as she rose from the kill to go tumbling in the snow. She seemed young again, a yearling pup, as she rolled over and over, long legs kicking now at air, now at the snow crust. Her eyes beckoned her mate, inviting him to share this snow bath. Soon he did. Afterwards they shook the powdery white from themselves and trotted away from the kill, seeking a new den in which to pass the day. Twice the bitch stopped and looked back at the remains of the kill, wondering if they should have buried it; but the snow was hard frozen, so she turned away each time. If other forest creatures finished the kill, the wolves would hunt again tonight. If not, they would eat of the carcass until it was gone.

Almost before the forest had hidden their shapes, the flutter of wings brought new sound to the scene of the kill and two gray and white birds plummeted from the top of a spruce. The gray jays had been waiting for the king beasts to be done with their meal and their frolic. Now they came to peck at the carcass, jaunty and hungry, tugging at this bit of meat or that lump of fat, between times making one of their many mimicking cries, their beady black eyes alert, their heads twisting this way and that, making sure that some other hunter did not come along to make a meal out of *them*.

Suddenly the jays squawked in unison and sped upwards, landing on the same branch that they had so recently left.

They scolded the newcomer, a vixen fox who had stepped lightly over a small dead spruce and sauntered towards the partly-eaten carcass. Her nostrils had picked up the tantalizing scent almost a quarter of a mile away. She had arrived while the wolves were eating, and had waited upwind, fearing the huge dog-creatures, until she was sure that they were far away from this place. She had watched them finish their meal and begin to play, and she had felt reassurance then, for she knew, as all wild creatures know, that when wolves have sated their hunger they will rarely attack again. The vixen was dainty as she pulled at the kill, crouching at the hindquarters of the deer, her coat a vivid chestnut glow in the sunlight.

Ten minutes later, while the fox was still eating, the gray jays flew down again. Like her, they knew that they were safe now. The fox ignored them. Five chickadees came also, perky little birds, the gymnasts of the forest, and they had their share, and the vixen let them be; for there was plenty for all. She was content, even though she was alone, because she, like the wolf bitch, had young in her belly. Yet deep within her was a vague sadness, which caused her to turn her head frequently away from the food to scan the forest behind her, as though in expectation. She was unconsciously looking for her mate, the now dead father of her unborn kits. The dog fox had stepped into a trap. It had fastened on his right leg and held him in agonizing, fearful frenzy while the vixen, powerless to help, had fled, his snarls of pain and fear acting like spurs upon her instincts, telling her to go, to take the unborn to safety.

This, too, is a rule of the wilderness, perhaps the prime rule of them all: the individual is expendable, but the species must be carefully guarded. Thus the dog fox died, but the pregnant vixen lived and would bear his young; so his kind would continue. But although the vixen had accepted this instinctively, she missed her mate. There was a tense, disquieting feeling within her mind that was fed by the memory of the dog's agonies. These had been so great, so frenzied, so terrifying that it would take much time to banish their effects. The fox had seen death many times — indeed, had inflicted it, for she herself was a killer; but death by tooth or claw is always swift. Not so when that demoniac thing had snapped at her mate's leg. It had lain in wait, silent. It had remained silent when it clamped its jaws on its victim. It had remained silent and indifferent to the snapping teeth of the dog fox. It had remained silent all that night, that thing of fear, maintaining its vice-grip on the lacerated leg. The dog had fought it. He had pulled at it, snapped at it, broken his teeth against its hardness. By dawn he had given up his struggles against it; he was almost exhausted, his fear less stark, his pain unendurable. He realized that the only way to freedom lay in the amputation of his own leg. Systematically he began gnawing his flesh and his bones, but he was slow, hampered by his broken teeth. And so he was still in the trap, and terrified anew, when the trapper came and dashed his brains out with an axe. The man was pleased. He estimated that he would get three dollars for the fox fur. He did not notice the agony still reflected in the dead eyes; he did not notice the signs of the creature's struggles, etched in the snow and the bushes around the trap. He saw the blood, and the white flecks of mangled brain, but only the three dollars held any meaning for him.

That evening, when the vixen passed by the scene of her mate's death, she had fled from it anew, terrified by the smell of his blood which mingled with the fearful scent of man. She had scuttled away and sought a new part of the forest.

And now she was eating, and when she was done she would seek a place of sanctuary for the night. Later, when the snows began to melt, she would look for a den in which to birth her kits.

It was a morning of clear, clean skies and warming sun. Little streams of crystalline water made music as they tumbled from high places and sought to soak into the partly-frozen earth. High in the blue above the forest, a wedge of Canada geese eased its way towards the north, the high-pitched calling of the birds clearly audible below. The wilderness was quickly changing to the time of new life, for March was spent and April was vigorous.

The wolves watched the forest from a place midway up the slopes of a sandy knoll. The early sun found reflection in their yellow eyes and danced gleaming on the white of their teeth. Visages that were ferocious during the hunt were now smiling and relaxed. The eyes were bright, alert, the mouths were open, the black lips parted in wolfish grins, the whole combining to belie the devilish reputation that these great beasts have acquired during centuries darkened by the ignorance of man. But man, the nemesis of the wild, was not there on that day, and the wolves were able to show the peaceful side of their nature.

In a gleaming spruce tree some ten paces from the wolves sat a red squirrel, little, furred body bunched upon a branch, bulbous black eyes lidded sleepily. The wolves knew that the squirrel was there; the squirrel knew that the wolves were aware of his presence. Yet he showed no fear. Of course, he was secure on his perch, out of reach of the fangs below, but there was more than that to his fearlessness. At another time he would have scampered chittering to the uppermost branches of his tree. Why, then, did he now show no fear?

The squirrel, like all other animals and birds of the wilderness, was an expert in sign. He knew when the cold was coming; he knew when the storm clouds gathered far away in the northland; he knew when the hawk was hunting, when the weasel slithered through the brush in quest of prey, and when the wolves were hungry. And now he knew that the pair of wolves were replete from their last kill. And knowing this, he feared them not. He dozed on his branch, enjoying the feel of warm sunshine once again.

The she-wolf yawned — a slow, lazy grimace that stretched wide her great jaws and revealed her fangs and teeth. Her mate turned and nudged her with his muzzle, then he licked her face. He opened his mouth two or three times in a half-yawn before giving vent to a huge gape that ended in a slight whine. These were signs of contentment and of affection. He licked her face again and she caressed his muzzle with her pink, moist tongue before she allowed her body to sprawl full length on the sun-warmed grass. The dog sat more straight upon his haunches, ears pricked forward, his gaze fixed on some point in the forest that only he could see. The bitch slept, snoring slightly.

The two had found this place shortly before March gave way to April. The female had approved of the location because it afforded a commanding view of the forest and because digging was easy in the sandy loam. At once she had set about remodelling the disused burrow of a fox, leaving her mate to his own devices. He was grateful for this, for she had been fussy over her choice of dens and they had travelled long and quickly in their search for a place in which to raise their litter. Now the male was free for a time. He could roam at will, sometimes hunting, as often as not just exploring his new range, etching upon his mind every bush and every tree; noting the places where the hares were plentiful, the watering stops of the deer, the small natural meadows where the mice lived, the beaver houses, the muskrat lodges. All these and more the dog noted during his lone forays into the forest. He sometimes ranged far, into new country, and on such occasions he might be gone for two or three days, while his mate worked on her burrow and now and then went on hunting trips of her own. These sorties were always short, usually netting for her a few mice, or a squirrel, or a muskrat.

The male was always solicitous and gentle with his mate. He never came home without bringing her meat from a kill. At times he might carry home a groundhog, the limp, reddish body swinging from his jaws. But sometimes, when a deer had been his prey, he brought the meat to her in his stomach, having gorged himself on the kill. He would stand before her, legs spread, bushy tail hanging loose, head down; he would retch three or four times and would disgorge from his stomach several pounds of still-fresh meat. The bitch would eat of this while he watched her, and after she had finished she would lick her chops clean and nuzzle into his thick neck, burying her nose in his still-heavy mane.

The she-wolf was big with her young and she was a little testy, snarling at her mate if he showed curiosity over her burrow — not viciously, but delivering a firm warning. The burrow was to be her domain until the pups were whelped and at least two or three weeks old. This was the way. Generations of female wolves had made it so and as many generations of males had respected it.

The dog was forbearing during his mate's time of trial. He was patient with her moods and conscientious in his work as a provider. His mate did not go hungry now that her time was near, and if now and then he felt impatience, if he found himself sometimes longing for her romping companionship, he did not show his feelings.

3

When Silverfeet was pushed from the comfort of his mother's womb onto the bare earth floor of the wolf den, the sun of late April was rimming the western horizon. One spear of rosy red light shafted through an opening in the forest and found the entrance to the burrow. It tinged the inner gloom with a suffused glow that made recognizable the shapes of four little wolves and gave distinction to the bulk of the fierce mother.

The she licked the birth sac from the body of her last born and Silverfeet whimpered, not understanding the newness that surrounded him. He was blind and wet and he feared the unknown that pressed upon him. But he found comfort in the soft, wet tongue that glided smoothly over his short puppy hair. There was comfort, too, in the acrid, dog-smell of the she; and there was promise in the sweet smell of milk that already trickled from her full dugs.

The she-wolf lay on her side, her body curled around her litter, and her heart was full of the great love that her kind have for their young. She finished cleaning her last cub. She snuffed at the other three. Then she nuzzled them gently, pushing them to the comfort of her nipples. One at a time the little wolves glued their blind faces to her, first a tiny, light gray bitch, then a black bitch, then a stubby, brindled male pup, and finally Silverfeet, the last born, but the biggest of the four. As the young nursed, the bitch lay placid, loving, her shaggy head hanging over her offspring, her yellow eyes etched in shiny relief by the dying sunlight that filtered into the underground den.

Outside, the father wolf sat guard. He had hardly moved for two hours, even when the squirrel scrambled down its tree and sat just above his head, churring and squeaking spite at the great hunter below. He merely raised his eyes once and stared at the cheeky mite, who immediately scuttled higher up the tree.

The big wolf watched over the forest. He was a shadow, a hump of dark substance that blended with the tree, a father wolf ready to kill any creature that threatened the safety of his mate and her young. He studied the forest. His eyes slid gracefully in their sockets as he scanned this and that, his senses forever on the alert, his triangular ears pricked bolt upright, fine radar scoops that could pick out and identify sounds breaking a great distance away.

A hawk circled lazily over the area of the den. The wolf did not worry about it, for it could offer no threat, but he watched it, perhaps instinctively, more likely because he found it interesting to observe the habits of the creatures that dwelt in his domain. The bird in the sky was a red-shouldered hawk, a stubby-winged, powerful predator that had been seeking the red squirrel that lived in the spruce.

Its intended victim had seen the hawk also and was hunched small in its den, a hollow in the tree trunk that had at one time been the home of carpenter ants, until the pileated woodpecker had come and had mined the protective bark and wood and made a hole through which its spear-like, bristly tongue had winkled out the ants. By the time the woodpecker had finished with the ants and their shelter, the tree had been breached, and when the squirrel found the hole the previous autumn he had gone to work with sharp teeth, enlarging the hole, scraping out the last of the rotting ant tunnels and remodelling their shelter into a den for himself. Now he cowered in his stronghold, secure from the hawk, yet afraid, so that he remained immobile.

But Silverfeet knew nothing of this. The little wolf was content in his dark world.

A mile away from the wolf den, to the south, the red vixen had also given birth. There were seven kits in the rock cave that she had found at the base of a low escarpment. They were ten days old when Silverfeet came into the world.

They were alone in the den next morning, for the vixen had gone hunting. She had not eaten meat for three days and the sucking young had taken strength from her body. She was hungry and lean and impatient for a kill, but she made herself travel with caution, appeasing the urgings of her belly with an occasional mouthful of spring grass. She smelled mouse, and in the gray light of daybreak, spotted the tiny creature as it scurried through last year's grasses in a desperate bid for safety. The vixen pounced . . . once . . . twice. She came down lightly, her questing paws flashing over the white-footed mouse. On the third jump she had the rodent; quickly it was chewed and swallowed, and she resumed the hunt, her hunger the more demanding now that it had been teased by this morsel of fresh meat.

The vixen continued her prowl, while the world into which her cubs had been born continued to awaken to spreading newness and life. A never-ending series of events and contours and shapes awaited the wolf pups and the fox kits who would have to learn about them, to study them as actively as man-children in a schoolroom, but with a need more pressing, for few mistakes are tolerated by the wilderness and those who are slow to master the lessons of life die quickly.

It was a big, busy world that awaited the young ones, a place of great trees, of bushes and grasses, of flowers and rocks and earth and water. Through the forest ran ancient game trails; there were lookout points, and scent stations; there were open places, of scant cover, that must be avoided by the hunting creatures; and there were places of good cover that allowed a hunter to hide and pounce and eat. There were other animals, and birds; some small, others large, all with definite habits which must be studied and learned if the young hunters were to survive. The forest was at once a classroom and a home, a place of safety and of danger, a region of famine and of food. But above all, it was a place confusing to the untried young things that were born into it.

Perched in a bone-dry pine sat a gray jay. He watched as the vixen passed under his perch, his head moving sideways so that he could focus one eye on the fox. The jay was interested. He knew that the vixen was hunting. He hoped that she would strike some creature too large to drag away or finish, for then there would be scraps for him to stuff into his ever-ready crop and perhaps there would be enough left over for his mate and the brood of young jays that were testing their wings in short flights around their nesting tree.

The gray jays nest early. His mate had started building during February, when the temperature hovered at thirty degrees below zero and the snows were piled high. The male had been content to let her build, watching while she wove the warm cup deep inside the shelter of a short, dense spruce tree. Now and then he went after some of the food that he had cached in the nooks and crannies of trees. Satisfying his own hunger first, he would ferry supplies to his busy mate, who snatched the food quickly and returned to her task, weaving together a mixture of moss and shredded bark, small sticks, and even wisps of matted spider's web, until she had concluded the structure to her satisfaction. When she sat in it, the cup had fitted her body perfectly, sealing in the heat of her brood veins which, criss-crossing her stomach, were swollen and throbbing with blood. One by one the female jay laid in the nest three grayish eggs, finely dotted with olive-brown. Patiently she sat, now and then shuffling her body and turning the eggs over, while her mate foraged in search of food and returned to her time and again to place some of it in her beak. Sixteen days later the eggs began to crack. At first it was the egg tooth of each chick that perforated the eggs, then the weight of the mother and her shuffling helped split the shells and three ugly, almost-naked nestlings wriggled and cried feebly within the shelter of the nest.

Until the baby jays became clothed in their insulating feathers the mother warmed them while the male bird provided for his family. He ranged far in search of food, carefully inspecting the peeling bark of dead trees for sleeping insects, spotting the remnants of kills left by the forest predators, picking at carrion, fat, bits of meat, anything that would sustain life in his mate and her chicks.

Today his hunting would be easier. The young jays were fully fledged and able to do some foraging for themselves, and his mate aided in the constant search for food. So he was content to follow the fox, and to wait for her to kill and perhaps leave him some scraps.

The vixen, meanwhile, had a scent strong and sweet in her nose. She stopped, her red body flattened, her ears pricked forward and her nose twitching. Somewhere ahead of her, hidden behind a rise in the land, was a groundhog. She moved forward with renewed stealth, and as she neared the hillock the grizzled, torpedo-shape of her quarry scampered over the rise.

The surprise was mutual. Both animals stopped instantly for a fraction of time. The groundhog realized his danger and turned to escape; the vixen flashed forward and quickly closed her fangs into the groundhog's short neck, clamping down hard and shaking at the same time. Both animals lost their footing and rolled down the far side of the hillock, the fox silent, the groundhog emitting strangled squeaks of fear. Suddenly it was over; the groundhog was dead.

The fox shook it once, twice, then settled to eat it. With the ease of practice she bit a hole in the soft underbelly and worked her pointed muzzle upwards, reaching for the choice parts, the liver, the heart, and the lungs. When these were gone she ate one haunch and part of the other. By this time the groundhog's body looked like a child's doll with half its stuffing removed. It was a limp bundle of bloodied fur that flopped this way and that as the fox worked on it. Presently she picked it up and turned towards her den, taking it to her cubs.

Halfway there she froze for an instant, then quickly pushed her supple body into the shelter of a deadfall spruce. She had heard and scented the male wolf as he set out on a hunt. The wolf passed some distance from the fox, but she remained immobile until she was sure he was gone.

In the wolf den the bitch fondled her pups, licking first one and then the other while they fed lustily with little grunts of pleasure.

In size and in looks, the pups resembled the young of a large domestic dog. Though their heads and faces were wolfish, their bodies were not. The long legs, handsome brush, and big feet of the wolf had not yet developed.

Two hours later the she pricked her ears forward, then arose quickly and stood expectantly by the den mouth. Soon she knew her mate was coming home; she could hear him, and by the slowness of his coming he was carrying fresh meat. Presently he emerged from the forest and her nose told her that he brought deer before her eyes saw the bloody haunch that was clamped between his jaws.

The she-wolf drooled. She stood outside the den, her front legs spread wide and forward, her haunches raised slightly, so that she appeared to be bowing. Her tail wagged and she whined; the sound was both a greeting and a reflection of her hunger. Her mate trotted towards her, eyes smiling, tail wagging, every move showing the pleasure that he felt — the pride of the primordial hunter bringing home food after a hard chase.

The dog deposited the deer meat in front of his mate, who

bent her head to smell it, then lifted it again to quickly lick the dog, a gesture of affection. Then she ate.

The sun was full risen. It had slid quietly over the trees, bathing the wolf den with the ruby of its first rays. Hazed by the gossamer of weak cloud, it looked flat and big, the colour of molten metal. In its light the shaggy wolf glowed with the hue of copper. The great teeth working on the deer flashed white, yet reflected the pinkness of the early light.

In his tree overlooking the feast, the squirrel soaked in the sunshine. Winter's long spell of cold and snow had starved his little red body, sapped from it the warmth of last summer's sun. Now he would replenish this life-giving element whilst he had the chance.

Once the bitch wolf looked up and eyed the squirrel, but there was more curiosity than savagery in her gaze. She licked her lips and pried some vestiges of meat from her gums, and her pink tongue flashed inside her mouth again as she lowered her head to take another mouthful of meat.

The dog, meantime, was sated; and he was tired. He sprawled by the den mouth, his ears cocked towards the feeble sounds of his offspring. The little wolves were crawling aimlessly around the nesting chamber, now and then chewing at each other's ears in the habit of all young animals.

The area around the den was a place of contrasts: on the ground the remnants of the wolf's kill; in the sky, the fullness of sun bathing the forest with new light and warmth; in the tree, the peaceful sleepy-eyed squirrel. On this April day there was beauty, there was savagery, there was wildness, there was love, there was young life. A butterfly floated down and landed on one of the scraps left by the she-wolf. The bitch watched as with slowly-moving wings the insect feasted royally on a morsel of meat. The drone of a bee broke the quiet of the scene; the insect, a scout seeking blooms and nectar, moved past the den and disappeared. A bird darted from a bush and settled on a shrub. It sang, the echoes of its melodious voice adding gladness to the scene.

The dog wolf yawned, stretching wide his cavernous mouth,

squinting his eyes, throwing his head back, the picture of contentment. His mate looked at him; he smiled. Then she arose and bellied her way into the den, to lie with her pups. The four cubs suckled until they could suckle no more, and then, one by one, they fell asleep, comforted by the presence of the great she-wolf who would defend them to her death.

Silverfeet was the last to finish — he was always the last. He seemed always to be hungry, but perhaps that was because he was the most active of them all. He was always exploring, always crawling, always chewing ears with his toothless gums, always poking into this corner or that. Already his mother had had to drag him back from the den entrance on several occasions. But today Silverfeet was hungry and lazy, and after taking his fill he found his favourite spot between the she's thighs. There, with his blunt little head hanging over one of her legs, he snored gently.

The bitch slept fitfully, her senses always on the alert for the slightest movement of any of her cubs, her head resting on her paws, her eyes now and then opening to form slits through which the shine of her pupils could be seen in the glow of the den.

Silverfeet was nine days old when his eyes began to open. The cubs were alone in the den that afternoon, for the bitch wolf had gone on a hunt with her mate. She had been forced by hunger to abandon the young ones. Had she been with a pack, she would not have gone and there would have been no hunger in the den; but although her mate was a good hunter he had been unable, alone, to bring down enough game for their needs. The dog had brought hares and groundhogs, and now and then a grouse, but such fare is meagre for two full-grown timber wolves, inadequate for a she-wolf nursing young. In the middle of plenty, these two efficient, powerful hunters were suffering want. Yet there was nothing really unusual about this. Wolves were created to hunt in packs; they are sociable animals that band together for survival. The dog and his mate, before the coming of the pups, had made an efficient, if small, hunting pack, but the dog alone could not hope to provide enough of the big game needed for the survival of the cubs. So the two had paired again and they had gone to hunt, perforce leaving the cubs unguarded.

Silverfeet and his brother and sisters were unaware of these things. They had nursed from their mother before she left the den, and now they made small dog-noises as they huddled together. Silverfeet had one of his black sister's ears clamped firmly in his mouth, and he was sucking it, comforting himself as a human baby might do with his thumb. At first, when the gummy lids of his right eye separated just a crack, exposing the eye to the sunlight that slanted into the cave, panic seized him and he let go of his sister's ear and tried to bury his head beneath the squirming bodies of the others. For some moments he continued to try to escape the light and then his second eyelid parted a little, chasing away more darkness. Fear was overcome by curiosity. Silverfeet withdrew his head from the bundle of living fur into which he had thrust it, and blinked owlishly towards the cave mouth. The strong light hurt his eyes and he turned away, but there was a fascination in that light. He had to stare at it. Slowly the pain of the light became less and less, until at last it left him altogether and for the first time he could see, though dimly.

That afternoon all the wolf pups gained their vision. Until then they had been guided by their ears and by their nostrils. They had crawled around and over one another, and had wandered aimlessly around the den chamber. Now they had eyes to guide them. They discerned each other for the first time and they recognized the smells and sounds of the den with their eyes. It was a wonderful experience. And if it frightened them at first, it held new promise.

The four rose to unsteady legs and peered at one another, smelling each other and sniffing about the chamber. They were small and feeble and their muscles would not co-ordinate properly, but the light drew them. Silverfeet was the first to make for it — slowly, wobbling, as often crawling as walking, but determined to reach the daylight that beckoned so persuasively. And the others followed. The four inched their way towards the outside on their short, rubbery legs, ignorant of the dangers that lurked there. Now and then one would sit down and rest a moment before setting off again.

Their progress was uneven but it took them closer and closer to their objective. Finally they were at the den entrance. Silverfeet stopped abruptly, dazzled by the sun. The others huddled around him, small, scared, and excited; four precocious animal children reaching too soon the great, green world. Silverfeet's chubby little body was toppled forward by the combined weight of the others. He rolled a little way outside, stopped, recovered, and scrambled slowly to his feet. He moved two steps forward, paused undecided, and peered back to see what the others were doing. The small gray bitch was just then moving, intent on following Silverfeet; the black bitch was sprawled flat on her belly at the cave mouth; the brindled little dog was still framed by the opaqueness of the cave, but he, too, was beginning to follow.

At last the four cubs were outside. They again huddled together, fear beginning to crowd their senses. They were so small and so unsure, and this new world was so big, even to their myopic sight. Silverfeet, not really knowing why, felt the urge to return to the safe darkness of the den and he began to walk again, but his senses were too weak and he did not know which way to go. Instead of retracing his steps, he moved farther away from the cave. His brother and sisters followed, a ragged little group that travelled but inches at a time. Some instinct warned Silverfeet that he was going in the wrong direction; perhaps the smell of the den became weaker in his nostrils, perhaps fear sharpened his senses. He stopped and the others stopped with him. They sat undecided.

The squirrel that lived near the den had been watching the young wolves. Squatting lazily on his nesting branch he had followed their ungainly progress from the cave mouth with the intent curiosity that all wild things display towards newness in their territory. Suddenly he sat upright and riveted his gaze upon an area of tangled scrubland a bare quarter of a mile from the den. The cubs continued with their antics, still trying to return to the security of their nursery.

The squirrel had lost all interest in them; his entire attention was devoted to the place he was watching. From his high vantage point he could see the brush moving. His keen ears caught a heavy sound coming from the area. Suddenly the squirrel chittered his alarm cry. He kept up the churring for perhaps half a minute, then he bolted up the tree and disappeared into his nesting hole. The cubs were oblivious of this. They heard the noise that the squirrel made, but they did not know that this was an alarm, alerting the forest to the presence of a dangerous prowler.

Silverfeet had succeeded in pointing himself in the right direction at last. Wobbling, he was slowly making his way towards the cave mouth. His sisters were following, but his brother had lost his bearings and was wandering farther away.

From the direction of the scrub patch a pig-like grunt disturbed the stillness of the afternoon. On its heels came the crackling of brush. Presently, the shaggy bulk of a black bear emerged into view. The bear's shambling course was erratic. He paused now and then to snuffle at something on the ground. Once he stopped at a dead log; with two slow smashes of his powerful forepaws, he tore it to pieces and stooped to lick up the ants from within the rotting wood, enjoying the pungent taste of the acidy bodies. When he had lapped up the last scurrying ant, he ambled up the hill towards the wolf den. Suddenly he stopped. Wolf scent had penetrated his nostrils. He was interested and cautious. He knew the smell of the wolf den, and he knew that in that den he could expect to find some young; these would be delicate mouthfuls for the still winter-hungry bear. But he knew also the savagery of timber wolves protecting their young, and so he paused, advanced a couple of steps, and paused once more, working his nostrils and flicking his ears, trying to locate the adult wolves. A few yards farther on he detected the smell of the cubs. He squinted, trying with his poor vision to locate their whereabouts, at the same time deciding that the parent wolves were not present. He quickened his steps, and the scent of the pups guided him unerringly towards the feebly-moving shape of the brindled male.

Returning home from a successful deer hunt, the parent wolves had picked up the scent of the bear. Now they were rushing towards the den, pausing occasionally to track the bear's progress, aware that he was heading directly for their den. The wolves were half a mile from home, but their progress was swift. They raced in their fastest gallop, jumping deadfalls, smashing their way through brush in an effort to get to their pups ahead of the marauding bear.

They burst out of the forest in view of their den just as the black bear seized the body of the brindled cub. The big bear stood on all fours, facing the cave entrance and eyeing the remaining pups. The little male was entirely hidden within his great jaws. He bit down, and the life was crushed from the little brindled body. At this moment two furious, savage things unleashed themselves upon the bear.

With flashing fangs and upcurled lips the wolves bore into the attack, smashing into the bear from either side. The bitch seized the bear's left hind leg, the dog sank his teeth into the hairy right flank. The bear whirled, shaking off both wolves with ease. He dropped the body of the pup. The wolves attacked again, their throaty growls of rage mingled with the bear's roar of surprise. The bear rushed the dog, trying to clasp him in his strong arms and crush him to death. While he was doing this the bitch struck him hard in the shoulder, knocking him off his feet. In a trice the dog wolf hit again and slashed a furrow in one of the bear's ears.

The bear was nimble. Quickly he regained his feet and charged the she-wolf; the tactic was repeated. While the she retreated out of reach, the dog bore in from the other side. Slowly the two wolves were easing the bear away from the cubs. The fight was fierce, and the noise of it filled the forest with fear. The three remaining pups, meanwhile, lay as though frozen, their instincts telling them to stay that way while the life and death struggle raged on; not even a whimper escaped them.

The bear was trying to run from the wolves now. Repeatedly he sought to gallop away, but each time he was met by one of the charging wolves. Again and again they bit at him. Time after time the bear tried to crush them. If he was slow with his biting jabs, he was fast with his forepaws. The fight seemed to have come to an impasse. But if the bear wanted to escape, the wolves wanted even more to get him away from the den.

Step by step, yard by yard, they drew him away, until at last they were down the slope and close to the brush out of which the bear had come. The dog had a wound on his right shoulder, where one of the bear's claws had raked him. Blood came, but the wound was not serious. The bear was bleeding from several bites, but these, too, were only superficial. His shaggy coat of matted hair made him almost impervious to the fangs of the wolves.

The wolves paused for a fraction of time, and the bear took advantage of the moment to wheel and charge into the heavy brush. The dog pursued him. The bitch hesitated, the mother instinct conquering her desire for vengeance. She climbed the slope to her pups.

She went first to the three, and smelled them and licked them, noting that they were unharmed. She turned to the dead cub then, licked it all over, and nuzzled it as though urging it to move. The bitch whined and licked her baby again. Carefully she opened her mouth and picked it up. It looked at first as though she were going to eat it, for the small body hardly protruded from either side of her jaws, but this is the way in which wolves carry their young. She turned and entered the den and deposited the dead pup in the nesting chamber. In a moment she was back outside, and one by one she carried her other pups to safety. She lay down with them, and Silverfeet and his sisters suckled from her. The dead pup lay on his back near her front paws; she nuzzled him and pushed him towards her dugs. She looked to the cave mouth and listened to the progress of the chase.

The dog wolf had no desire now to attack the bear, but he kept chasing him, pushing him out of his country, always near but never actually closing with him. They ran in this fashion for about two miles. At last the dog stopped. The bear kept travelling, grotesquely agile, looking like a moving black ball as he raced top speed to disappear over a hilltop. The dog waited a few moments and listened, and when he could hear the bear no more he turned and raced for home.

When he arrived at the den, his mate greeted him at the entrance. She whined, and licked at the blood on his shoulder, cleaning the wound. He caressed her muzzle with his tongue. They stood silent for a time, until the bitch whined again. They both felt a great uneasiness. Their den had been discovered, their pups attacked. They would have to move.

In the she-wolf's memory was a place that she had inspected before she had found her present den. This first location was a hollow under the bell-like root of a fallen balsam tree, which had at one time served as a fox den. This place, she knew, could easily be enlarged and although it was not as good a den as the one she had, still it offered shelter and concealment. To this place she would eventually move her young, but not tonight. She needed time in which to make up her mind.

She left her mate at the den mouth, entered the cave and again lay with her pups. The dog, tired after his hunt and his fight, flopped down in front of the den, as uneasy as his mate. For some time his senses remained on edge and he kept sniffing the wind, raising his head high to suck in the odours of the forest. Eventually, when no disturbing scent came to him on the breeze, he let his head slump on his paws, closed his eyes, and slept.

Inside the den, the mother wolf was licking the inert body of her dead pup. Silverfeet and his sisters had nursed and were sleeping; they were curled up against the warm protection of her belly fur. The she had the dead pup between her forepaws, and she licked it constantly, while nuzzling it and moving it from one side to the other. An occasional soft whine told of her distress.

Outside the sun was sinking. The animals and birds of the forest were still uneasy. The red squirrel emerged from his den only to dive back into it again and to peer from it fearfully. The birds were strangely silent. The fury of the fight had cast a spell upon this section of the forest — a spell that would last until the morning, when a new sun and a new day came to break it.

Next morning the other creatures that lived near the wolf den had recovered from the death of the previous day. But not the wolves. Both adults were still uneasy, especially the bitch. She and her mate had hunted well yesterday; they had pulled down an aging buck deer and had come home replete from the kill. But if their stomachs were still round from the gorge, their senses were stretched taut, their instincts honed fine. They could not settle. Twice the dog went to enter the den chamber. Each time he was driven away by his mate, her savage growls a warning to be heeded, for during her time of distress she made no distinctions. She was there to guard her young and this she would do, even against her mate.

The dog accepted her anger. He was, as all hunters must be, a philosopher. If opportunity did not come today, it would come tomorrow or the next day; if his mate was made savage this morning because of the bear's attack, she would, in due course, become her old self again. Time heals all things, and the dog resigned himself to this period of disquiet. This is the way of the wild. This is the way that all creatures must be when their days are divided between starvation and plenty, between danger and comfort.

The dog himself was uneasy. As yet the tiny pups awoke in him little more than an instinct of protection. But his den had been ravaged; an enemy had come and had been fought and had retreated. This kind of memory lasts in the wilderness. It must last, for those who forget die, and those who learn from their experiences live to beget of their kind.

The dog ambled away to the scene of yesterday's kill. There he fed again, and when he had finished he seized a partly-gnawed haunch of the deer and carried it to the den. Outside the cave mouth he whined once, and dropped the meat. He retreated a few steps and settled to watch. Presently the bitch emerged, looked the dog full in the eyes, picked up the meat and disappeared into the darkness of her den. The dog yawned. He composed himself for sleep, curling his leanness into a ball, his colouring blending into the contours of the land and into the shade cast by the squirrel's tree. Soon he slept.

The sun of May was benign, a gentle warmth that permeated all things in the forest. It warmed the wolf, filling him with a pleasant drowsiness. He slept for three hours. And while he slept, the life of the forest went on. The insects were busy, each with its own small task; the birds, many of them already nesting, filled the forest with their voices, preening or feeding within spruce or poplar or balsam.

Planing circles through the cloudless sky a red-shouldered hawk surveyed his hunting ground. His mate was sitting on three eggs in the nest that the two had built deep in the crotch of a tall poplar tree. The male was seeking prey. His mate had to be fed.

As he flew over the trees he dipped in a swift half-glide that was almost a dive. He vanished inside the canopy of forest and set his wings to glide, steering between the trees with his broad tail as though controlled by radar. Suddenly he rose slightly, and came gently to rest on a branch of his plucking tree, a dead birch that grew in a hollow, surrounded by tall spruces. On the ground at the foot of this tree were the remnants of the hawk's recent kills; feathers, squirrel fur, and the pastel hairs of a chipmunk. This tree served the hawk both as vantage point from which to scan for prey and as a place to bring his victims to be plucked expertly by his hooked beak.

This morning he sat quietly, his body unmoving, his head turning slow circles while his keen eyes detected every movement in the area. He spotted a quick scurrying amongst the dead leaves. A chipmunk trotted jauntily and carelessly in search of food. The hawk swooped swiftly downwards with outstretched claws. The chipmunk gave a shrill squeal and tried frantically to dodge away from the grasping legs. In vain. One taloned foot reached down swiftly and its rapier claws gaffed the body of the chipmunk. Already the hawk was rising with his wriggling victim gripped inexorably. Up onto the plucking tree flew the hawk. He landed on a branch still gripping the struggling, squealing chipmunk. With one swift lunge of his beak, he pierced the rodent's brain. The chipmunk shuddered once, twice; then it lay still.

The hawk began to pluck his prey. The fur floated down softly, a silent requiem to a small forest creature that had been careless and had paid for its mistake with its life. Soon the body of the chipmunk was naked. The hawk flew off his perch, gripping the food in his right leg, and carried it to the female sitting on the nest. The hawk whistled once, a slurred two-syllable victory cry, as he braked with broad, stubby wings and landed on the edge of the nest. The female reached up swiftly and grasped the still-warm body proffered by her mate. For a moment the male watched as the female tore into the flesh. Then he went off to glide once more through the forest, this time in search of food for himself.

Morning gave way to midday. The sun was a ball of fire suspended overhead, casting only small shadows. Inside the wolf den the bitch awoke and yawned, lifted her hindquarters and stretched, yawned again. As she completed her stretch, her whole body, taut and tense, quivered slightly before relaxing into normalcy. She turned to her pups who were asleep cuddled to each other. She licked them and nosed them a little, but the young wolves were sleepy and did not respond to her caresses. One whimpered; it was hard to know which one it was, for the sound eased its way out of the lupine bundle. The bitch tarried over her young for a moment before walking slowly to the entrance of the den, there to pause, her head and shoulders protruding outside. She looked at her sleeping mate. Instantly his eyes opened wide and he returned her glance. No sound was exchanged between them, but the male got up and moved closer to the den. Sitting by it, he yawned and stretched as the she had done, and afterwards nibbled gently at her shoulder. Then he squatted flat upon his haunches, mouth agape, his breath coming quickly, for it was hot and the panting cooled his body.

The female turned and re-entered the den and when she came out again she carried Silverfeet, the small pup almost entirely hidden in her mouth. She had decided to move to the new quarters. The male wolf would stay and guard the remaining pups while she carried the first to the new place.

Half an hour later the bitch was back and this time, when she emerged from the den, she carried the black pup. One by one the pups were taken to their new quarters, the male joining his mate on the last trip. Inside the abandoned den the body of the dead pup was already decomposing, filling the cavern with the rank-sweet odour that proclaims carrion.

4

On both sides of a wide ravine scaly-barked jack pine dominated that area of the forest in which the wolves had made their
summer home; but in the ravine itself, where the bitch had
settled her family, cedar and balsam jostled each other for
growing room, darkening the forest with their wide skirts. The
trees formed tight clumps, some pure stands of cedar, others
mixed stands of cedar and balsam. Here and there in that otherwise dry ravine was an open, wet place holding a few shaggy
alders and willows. Ferns were everywhere, the heavy fiddle-
heads which grew three feet tall, and beneath these, tiny forest
creatures scurried fearfully in pursuit of their living.

Within the denseness of each clump of mature trees the forest floor was almost bare. Here and there, patches of thick moss offered bedding places for the wolves; but mostly the brown earth was carpeted only with fallen needles and dead branchlets. The root under which the bitch had fashioned a new home for her young was ancient: it belonged to a long-dead balsam tree that had been smashed out of its growing earth by a wild autumn wind. Its stark, interlaced roots stretched their brown, bony fingers upwards, some still clutch-ing stones and clumps of dried earth. The once massive trunk was rotten and eroded by tunnelling things: mice, insects, squirrels. All these, since the wolves had come, had either left the area or fallen prey to the needle fangs of the pups, who were now eight weeks old and full of boundless energy.

It was late June. The days were long and warm, and the nights pleasantly fresh, offering coolness to the animals and birds of the forest. But the mosquitoes and black flies were in full season and the young wolves showed signs of their bites on their noses and within the hollows of their ears; bloody spots and reddening bumps, where the pests had injected an irritating fluid to thin the blood of their victims, the better to suck it through their stinging mouthparts.

With the stoic endurance of all wild creatures, the young wolves withstood the constant attacks of their tormentors, brushing them away with a paw, or twitching an ear or a muscle to shake off a more than usually persistent pest. Occasionally they would sit on their haunches and scratch vigorously at one of the itching places.

The parent wolves left the pups alone often now that their young were old enough and fleet enough to escape the few dangers that the forest held for them. There was need for meat to feed the family, for the bitch was weaning the pups. Occa-sionally she would allow them to nurse, but more and more often she discouraged them, leaving them behind while she went with the dog on serious hunting trips.

When the parent wolves returned from such trips their bellies were rounded with fresh meat and the pups forgot their desire to nurse as they crowded eagerly for the food which they knew their parents would disgorge for them. Usually the arrival of the hunting wolves was announced some distance from the rendezvous by a soft howl or two. As soon as the ululating moan filled the forest air, the pups pricked up their ears and set their faces in the direction of the howl. Within seconds each small mouth opened, each squat head was raised, and each black, shiny nose was directed at the sky. In almost-unison their young voices intoned the wolf song, treble imitations of their parents' calls. Then the pups would rush in the direction of the hunters, adults and young would meet in some tangled, brushy place, and the feeding ritual would begin.

The pups would bite at the muzzles of the adult wolves until, stimulated by the soft nips, they began to disgorge the still-fresh meat that they had carried home so conveniently in their stomachs. The small wolves thrust their muzzles into the parents' mouths, and as the meat came up they seized it greedily and gulped down the raw, red food. There was always plenty for all, but Silverfeet could never seem to accept this. Being the strongest and the largest of the three cubs, he was almost always the first to reach his mother or father, whichever of the two happened to be in the lead, and he bit harder than the others, bringing on quickly with his puppy teeth the parental urge to disgorge.

Silverfeet was starting to look like a wolf. He now weighed seventeen pounds, and he had the outlines of his parents: the sharp, arrow-shaped ears, the slanted, yellow-amber eyes, the broad forehead, and the long muzzle that would one day develop the power to crush the leg bones of moose, elk, and deer. He was a beautiful, lithe wild thing, young and playful, a healthy whelp of the forest who had little time for seriousness and who must always be on the move, always inquisitive, poking at this and that, leading his two sisters into new areas and constantly exploring. He managed more often now to catch small things: mice, young hares, even insects.

Silverfeet's coat was dark gray, almost charcoal in colour, peppered with lighter guard hairs which gave him a grizzled look and set off his silver-white legs and feet. His black sister was considerably smaller, but just as active. She shone a glossy ebon in the sunlight and the white splash on her chest was startling within the blackness of her coat. Her eyes were as active and vigilant as her brother's, just as full of life and just as full of mischief. But the small, light gray bitch was ailing. She was always the last to eat and she did not respond fully to the stimulus of food or to the playful promptings of her brother and sister. Increasingly she lay down and refused to join the others in their endless games, her yellow eyes dull, her flanks pinched, her hair dry and brittle.

While Silverfeet and his black sister had been given the boundless strength and energy of nature, she had been marked for an early death. This is the way that nature keeps balance amongst her subjects. Always, and to every species, there are born more young than the forests can sustain; and always some of these young are doomed. The small wolf had been invaded by deadly bacteria which man, had he been able to examine her, would have called *listeria*. These invisible flecks were coursing through the gray pup's bloodstream, invading every corner of her body, weakening her so that she would not compete with the others, making her feel more keenly the effects of the blood-sucking flies. Inertia, lack of appetite, and the disease within her would soon cause her death and so, while Silverfeet and the other pup romped joyfully and staged their mock battles, the little gray bitch slept listlessly in the shade of the root that was her home.

One morning early, when Silverfeet was exploring a small natural clearing some little distance from the den, the buzzing of powerful insect wings attracted his attention. His keen eyes, aided by his magnificent sense of hearing, soon located the flier. It was a giant waterbug, a brown, two-inch-long predatory insect that was winging its way from its customary pond in search of a mate. The bug landed in a clump of grass a few yards away. The young wolf bounded over to it, ears erect and pricked forward, eyes showing the keen anticipation of the hunter. In a moment he straddled the insect, reached down with open mouth, and picked it up. Instantly he let it go and brushed at his lips with a paw, trying to appease the hurt that the waterbug's powerful stinger had inflicted. If Silverfeet had been a domestic dog pup, that would have ended the encounter and he would have run from the place, tail tucked between his legs, venting his hurt with a high-pitched yelp. But this is not the stuff of the hunting wolf. Silverfeet was nonplussed, but only for a moment. Ignoring the hurt, he pounced again, now smashing with a powerful paw at the heavy brown body. As quickly, he reversed his tactics and again opened his mouth and seized the insect. This time his sharp teeth pierced the chitinous armour of the monster bug. But its taste was unpleasant and he spat it out. Silverfeet regarded his prey, cocking his intelligent head first to one side, then to the other. Eventually, he decided that what could not be eaten should certainly be rolled on, especially when it tasted so bitter. Allowing his left front leg to go slack, bringing his neck and shoulders down and pushing with his back legs, he managed not only to squash the bug but to smear its body juices along his neck and flank. He rose on all fours and sniffed at the mangled corpse. The tangy smell invited more rolling and he dropped on his side and rolled over and over on the insect, smearing his body with its smell.

His actions were instinctive, dictated by the unconscious need of the predator to mask his own scent with the odour of other things. Just as avidly would the wolf roll on the decomposed remains of some dead creature, or upon the excreta of bear or wolverine, or upon dank, rotting vegetation left at the water's edge by beaver or muskrat. Young hunters must quickly learn the tricks that will ensure survival, and Silverfeet and his black sister were no exception. Learn or perish, says nature; those who learn, live, and those who do not, die. Thus only the finest specimens of each kind continue to supply life to the wilderness.

Now Silverfeet spotted movement in the grass ahead. He trotted to it and nosed a snake into the open. The harmless garter snake coiled and struck at its tormentor, discharging from its anus a vile-smelling liquid. Silverfeet had no care for the reptile's puny jaws. Again and again the small, serrated teeth of the insect-eater fastened feebly on his nose, drawing tiny drops of blood, but Silverfeet just shook his head and the snake flew off to be pounced on again, swiftly, by the young wolf. The game lasted several minutes and would have gone on longer had the black bitch not come up and joined her brother. Between the two, each competing for the prize, the snake made good its escape, slithering under a small pile of rocks from which it could not be dislodged. But the wolves were undismayed. Sprinkled over the grasses of the area were liberal quantities of the snake's strong liquid and each pup rolled in it, Silverfeet adding to his body the pungent smell of snake.

When the rolling was over, Silverfeet decided that a wrestling match with his sister would divert him. She was standing sideways to him; he eyed her speculatively for a moment, then charged, striking her roughly with his right shoulder and bowling her off her feet. In a trice he was onto her, growls of mock anger coming from his throat as they rolled over and over, slashing playfully at each other with their razor teeth. Once Silverfeet clamped his teeth on one of his sister's ears; she squealed her pain and the snarl that ended her cry contained anger. Silverfeet let go his hold and bounded to his feet, facing her, his front legs spread out, his shoulders and head lowered, his mouth agape, the gleam of mischief in his eyes. Undismayed by the warning growl that escaped her, he charged again. But she was ready for him this time. She sprang right over him and his rush ended in an ungainly tumble followed by the flashing body of his sister, who sought to take advantage of his fall. She seized him by the loose skin of his back, but he twisted agilely and swiftly and got her by the scruff of the neck. Both rolled and tumbled, growling fiercely but playfully as they indulged their pent-up energies in a game that was yet not a game, because the exercise and the experience of infighting which they were now gaining, would help them when they were adult bush marauders, exposing themselves to the dangers of the hunt.

They played, and their games were akin to the war training of young men. But their gray sister watched them now and then with her dulled gaze and remained curled under the shelter of the old root — listless and sick.

As abruptly as the wrestling bout had started, it ended. Silverfeet, the challenger, broke off contact. His keen eyes had once more spotted movement nearby. This time it was a large bullfrog; a fat, slow-hopping creature returning to its breeding pond. Silverfeet pounced. But with growing caution he did not immediately attempt to seize the frog. Instead he lowered his head and began to sniff it. Just at this moment the frog jumped. The move caught Silverfeet by surprise. He ducked and jumped backwards, wary but not afraid.

This was Silverfeet's first frog. He was intrigued by this new creature that did not scurry fearfully away but sat seemingly placid until the wolf's nose was almost touching it, only to jump away just as it was about to be nudged. Silverfeet watched the frog for a few moments. It sat still. The pup advanced towards it, stiff-legged and cautious; the frog did not move. Silverfeet entered into the spirit of what, to him, appeared to be a new and exciting game. This time he bounded back, but quickly darted forward and sought to grasp the frog in his mouth. Hop — and the creature was two feet away. Yelping with excitement, Silverfeet chased it and this time, moving faster, his nose touched the bullfrog's back. The contact furnished a nerve-tingling shock and the young wolf sprang away, a touch of panic seizing him. This strange, hopping thing was not only cold, it was actually wet, and its scent was like nothing he had encountered. It reminded him of the beaver dam where he went with his parents to drink now and then; it had the same water-odour, and yet it was different. He watched the frog for a moment, a speculative look in his eyes. Repeatedly he nudged it with his nose, risking its cold wetness, but not quite daring to open his mouth and take it.

After a time he began to get bored. He paused and looked for his sister. When he saw her high-stepping through long grass with tail held erect and ears pricked forward, a bright gleam fixed in her slant eyes, he abandoned the frog and raced towards her, eager to get into the hunt for the mice which he knew she had scented.

The two pranced on stiff legs through the grass, the delicious smell of the rodents strong in their nostrils. Silverfeet pounced once, twice. His paw felt something warm and wriggling and he pressed down. Then, swiftly, he withdrew his foot and lowered his muzzle all in one smooth action, and when he lifted his head the tail of a mouse protruded from his jaws. At once his sister went for him, but he turned his back on her, and chewing twice, perfunctorily, he swallowed the tasty morsel whole. The small black pup turned away and soon she, too, had found a mouse and eaten it. Both pups spent the next fifteen minutes hunting through the long grass, but no more mice rewarded them. And now they could hear the call of the parent wolves.

At once both pups tensed, their bodies quivering with excitement, their noses testing the wind in the direction from which the howls had come. The calls were repeated. The pups lifted their heads and replied, their young voices thin and querulous, contrasting with the deep, throaty tones of the adults. Now silence. The pups waited a moment, still quivering with anticipation. Silverfeet bounded forward, his sister close behind, and the pups raced wildly and happily through the forest, the thought of fresh meat spurring them to madcap enthusiasm.

The gray pup whined but did not move.

This time the parent wolves did not carry the meat in their stomachs. They had killed a deer, a white-tail buck who had been unable to maintain the speed with which he had been endowed in his prime. The wolves had cut down the distance as the faltering buck fought against the botfly maggots that clogged his breathing passages. In vain he tried to suck air into his labouring lungs. At last the dog put on a spurt, came up alongside his quarry and, with a quick sideways lunge of his shoulder, neatly tripped the deer. With a twist the dog reached for the throat, while the she bounded on top of the buck and deftly disembowelled it. The deer was dead in moments. The wolves fed well; as if by mutual consent, each gnawed away at a haunch, cracking easily through the bones. Now they carried some back to the rendezvous, for the pups must exercise their jaws.

When the two young wolves met their parents they became frantic at the sight and smell of meat. But the adults kept their hold on the food in spite of the jumping, whining, tearing pups, and raced on towards the rendezvous, unwilling to drop the meat until all three pups had a chance at it.

When the old root was reached the she allowed Silverfeet to wrench the partly-eaten leg from her mouth. The pup dragged it away, seeking sanctuary within a clump of balsam, and his black sister copied his actions. But the small gray bitch made no move to capture her share. The mother went to her and disgorged some of the meat that she had eaten. The gray pup sniffed at the food but made no attempt to touch it. The bitch whined and reached out and caressed her whelp with her tongue, licking her all over, nudging her with her nose. The gray pup did not respond. She was dying; and by morning her stiffened body lay alone under the root, its flesh an invitation to the carrion-eaters of the forest.

July came furnace hot, its turgid breath seeming to banish every cloud from the vast blue sky that framed the incandescent fire of the sun. The days were humid and still; the nights were alive with the droning of mosquitoes. That year it was a month infernal, engulfing the wilderness with its feverish breath, a month of almost volcanic evil that scorched the very earth, dried the sap in the trees, emptied the beaver ponds and sucked life's moisture out of streams and rivers.

The animals and birds of the wilderness sensed the danger of this time, and were restless and nervous. Some, the lesser ones, were forever ready to escape, their bodies gripped by taut nerves that would propel them into instant, frantic action. Others, like the wolves, were uneasy, too, but found value in this fervent month, for its heat had sapped the energy from many creatures and the hunting was good.

It was dawn during the fourth week of the month; a still, hot daybreak alive with the scream of mosquitoes, now and then punctuated by the buzzing of the dragonflies that forever sought to prey upon them. The sun had inched its way over the eastern trees, a molten rind of orange with rays of lavender, yellow and red that set the forest a-sparkle. The scene was beautiful — deadly beautiful. Even the wolves felt the threat that lingered over this day. The parents were uneasy as they sat on a rocky knoll and surveyed their world; the pups, Silverfeet and his black sister, did not play, but shared the nervousness of their parents. Below the rock lay what was left of last night's kill, an emaciated fawn. The flies were busy with the carcass.

The wind fanned from the northwest, where a thin, gray-black finger lanced evilly at the sky, a waving, fragile finger perhaps four miles distant from where the wolves sat. The she-wolf stared at it for a little time, then she whined. There was fear in her voice. She knew the meaning of that skeletal black wraith: fire had come to the wilderness.

The four wolves stood up and watched the streamer of smoke. They saw it gain in volume, become blacker, spread itself from a finger to a column, from a column to a mushroom, from a mushroom into a long, ragged wall that started to advance rapidly in their direction.

Soon the orange of flame was visible. Now and then, as though unseen volcanoes had erupted, quick explosions sent red sparks high into the air. The fire grew and gained momentum, veering more directly towards the place where the wolves stood. Its roar was clear, an ominous thundering that inspired fear primordial.

Terror gripped the wolves; the panic that their ancestors must have felt at similar sights and sounds welled from deep within them. They howled their anguish, four voices bespeaking fear. The bitch broke. Taking one last look at the advancing wall of flame, she tucked her tail deep between her legs and turned her face to the rising sun. She ran, and her pack ran with her.

As they fled, they were flanked by other forest dwellers. The vixen fox, her cubs at her heels, ran for a time near the pack. Snowshoe hares bounded madly ahead, uncaring about the wolves. Once, four white-tailed deer passed within yards of the pack, but never a glance did the fleet stags bestow upon their greatest enemies. The creatures of the forest were not at war today; the fire had seen to that. Instead it was as though all the forest life was united in a common goal: to escape from the roaring inferno that galloped at their heels.

The smoke was with them, its pungent smell and dark, motile body the threat of what would follow. The wolves redoubled their speed. So did the other creatures. Some died running, their minds so full of panic that they crashed headlong into the trunks of trees. None stopped to examine the dead. Even hungry predators passed them by. Food was forgotten. All things were forgotten. Except fear. This stark spectre dominated them all.

The fire roared like some mighty, wounded beast. From its maw came ash and sparks, quick-rising, infernal offspring that were fanned forward by the heat to fall, hungry, on other parts of the forest, and there create their own holocausts.

The staccato crack of splitting, tortured wood added percussion to the terror; the sudden, roman-candle-like flare of newly-ignited birch trees lent fury to the kaleidoscopic hell that had been unleashed upon the wilderness.

In the path of the flames sat an owl. The bird was confused: fear had robbed it of direction. The big gray bird rocked on its branch, attempted to see through the thickening smoke, hesitated. At last it took flight, but it was too late. The air had become searing hot. Twenty feet from its tree the owl's primary feathers shrivelled at their ends, curled, and became black blobs. The bird plunged into the fire and was engulfed.

A she-bear tried to coax her twin cubs to hurry. The young ones had been scorched and they kept stopping to drag their round, fat rumps over the hot ground in an effort to appease the sting of their burns. The mother grunted at them, ran ahead a short way, then turned and retraced her steps. Fear motivated her next actions. She growled threateningly, took two swift steps towards one cub, and cuffed it vigorously with a huge forepaw. The cub screamed. Then she cuffed her second cub and it too screamed. Nothing could hurry these terror-stricken bush babies, not even the fury of their mother, who, until that day, had always inspired obedience in their small minds. The she-bear stopped, at a loss. Alone she could have saved herself, but death was inevitable if she stayed with her cubs. She chose to stay and, powerless, she reacted to the fire in the only way that she knew. She roared her fear and anger, and charged into it. She died quickly. Moments later the relentless flames passed over the seared bodies of her cubs.

Small things shrieked in the burning grass. Mice, shrews, moles screamed their agonies and then lay still and the fire passed over them and left small blobs of smoking black where there had once been life. An aging lynx stumbled as fast as his senile body would allow. He looked back often, stark terror in his amber eyes. But he was too slow. The heat reached him first, suffocating him, and this was merciful, for when the fire burned into his fur and flesh he was already dead.

The fire reached the edge of a small beaver pond, consuming all its vegetation before the flames were split by the water and coursed on, surrounding the pond. In the water many beasts had taken refuge, some clinging to floating, peeled poles, others just swimming in frantic aimlessness, a few sitting huddled on the beaver lodge. They all died, even the beaver inside their home. The pond was small; the fire boiled its water, scalding to death those that it could not incinerate.

Ahead of the fire ran the wolf pack, swiftly, tirelessly, panic dominating their instincts. They ran south, unheeding where their pumping legs were taking them. And almost as swiftly roared the fire.

Its heat already touched the wolves. They began to slow as their lungs choked on the hot air and smoke, and on the fine ash that showered on them.

Then, blessedly, came a swift river.

Into it the she-wolf led her pack. In a moment the wolves were caught by the current.

Downstream they went, struggling for life against this new threat, yet feeling the coolness of the waters, unafraid of this mad-rushing, twisting watercourse that carried them away from the merciless fire.

The two men squatted beside a patch of damp, muddy ground, scrutinizing it intently. One, middle-aged, seamed of face and casual in dress, was slowly wiping mud from a hand that was obviously at home with farm chores; the other, younger, leaner, wearing hip-clinging jeans and checkered shirt, was still probing with a bony finger at something etched in the mud. He turned to the farmer.

"Yeah . . . they're wolf tracks. Fresh, too." He emphasized his last remark by stabbing again at the mud. "I'd say two old ones an' two cubs."

The older man rocked on his heels, scratching reflectively at his thinning hair.

"What're you goin' to do?" His question was laconic.

The other was silent for a moment. His fingers were absently caressing the pad marks so clearly defined in the mud. There was a distant look in his eyes, which were directed to the woods at the far end of the farmer's clearing.

"Could use strychnine, but that mightn't work. Sure would love to trap them pups alive, though."

The farmer stared at his companion. He frowned, thinking. When he spoke his voice was harsh.

"What would you want to live-trap them varmints fer? Kill 'em, that's what you're paid fer. Next thing, they'll be into the sheep."

The trapper shook his head slowly.

"I don't think you've got much to worry about. The fire put those critters out of the bush and down here. The way I see it, they're already heading back north," he said.

"What about my sheep, though? Suppose they kill some for me?"

"Listen," the lean man spoke softly. "I can get a hundred bucks for each one of those pups, if I can trap 'em alive. Dead, I just get a few bucks. Besides, I'm sure they're heading outa here."

"Well, they better be, is all!" The farmer spoke angrily.

"Tell you what. I'll keep an eye on your sheep for the next week or so. If I see wolf tracks around your place, I'll put out poison. O.K.?"

The other nodded grudgingly and the two turned their backs on the tracks, pausing to talk a while longer before leaving the river area.

Against her will the bitch wolf had been driven by the forest fire into man-country. She was uneasy.

When the four exhausted animals had climbed out of the river at a point where the watercourse made a wide turn and slowed its violent flow, there had been only one thought in her mind: they were safe from the fire.

From where she and her pack stood dripping on the river-bank she could still see the pall of smoke that darkened the northwestern skyline, but instinct told her that the inferno was not now coming in her direction. So she stood on the grassy bank and intuitively debated her next action while sucking great gulps of pure air into her smoke-sore lungs. She stood head down, mouth agape, straining at the flanks. She was sore and battered, bleeding in several places where driftwood branches had gouged her in the downriver ride. So, too, stood her mate and their pups. They made a tableau, these four mauled forest hunters, standing on the riverbank, soaked, bloody, exhausted.

As usual, the pack waited for the bitch to make the decisions, for she was the most experienced and she had always led well. And to her keen nose the scent of man, an enemy more dreaded even than fire, was strong. So she turned and looked to the shelter of the forest that was perhaps a quarter of a mile away, on the other side of a lush green field.

She led. The others came in single file. Their steps were slow, for pads were raw and muscles were stiff, but it was the best pace they could muster. Luck had been with them that day. They had lived while many others had perished. If their luck held for just a little longer, long enough to allow them to cross the open field and fade into the forest before the eyes of man could see them, all might yet go well.

The she-wolf had forgotten the tracks. She had not, in fact, even given them a second thought. Wolves, like all predators, hunt by scent or sound, or by actual sight of their quarry. Signs without scent mean nothing to them. Thus the tracks, being their own, were just a part of the riverbank; they held no meaning.

Man alone, of all the predators, uses the sight of tracks to guide him in his hunting. But this the she-wolf did not know.

5

Two months had passed since the fire had driven the wolves into man-country and the bitch, wisely, had kept her pack hidden in the forests that fringed this small settlement area. She had always led them after wild game, remembering the slaughter she had witnessed when her first pack had been rash enough to attack man's creatures. So the farmer lost none of his sheep. He had forgotten about the wolves.

Not so the hunter. He had spent weeks following their progress, had been near them now and then, and had listened as the pack spoke during the full moon. Now he felt he could achieve his purpose. He began to plan.

The scarlet maples brushed bold colour into the canvas of early autumn. September had been, and still was, a benign month, gentle and fresh, an insect-free time that filled the two young wolves with a joyous excitement that bordered on hysteria. They had learned to hunt, and took pride in their marauding journeys with their parents, helping in the long chases when deer was the prey. Often they ventured alone to stalk and pounce upon groundhogs or hares, and to indulge themselves with the tiny bodies of mice and moles, which afforded them much sport and refined their predatory instincts.

Frequently, while the bitch and her mate rested replete and content within some cool, shaded bower, the six-months-old pups prowled unhungry in search of mice. Guided by their extraordinarily keen noses they quartered the forest floor, moving easily, heads up, pointed ears erect and swivelling in a constant search for the small rustling noises that the mice made as they skittered through their grassy tunnels.

The young wolves were more than half grown now. They were lithe, beautiful in an ungainly, puppy way, and powerful. The needle-like milk teeth were falling out and being replaced by the strong, gleaming white teeth of adulthood. Though not yet fully developed, these were still fearsome weapons, powered by broad mandibles and tough jaw muscles. The pups' coats held the glistening sheen of healthy life, the outer guard hairs grown long, the silken underfur already thickening in preparation for the oncoming freeze.

Autumn was their testing time and they seemed to know it. During the final weeks of this season Silverfeet and his sister must pass their last trials, like students who are about to sit for final exams. But there was no room for failure in the classroom of the young wolves. Failure for them meant death, and, sensing this, the pups flung themselves wholeheartedly into the business of living. They were hardly ever still, always restless, forever alert to the hunt. Now and then, when both pups went after the same prey, short, snarling fights ensued over the body of the victim until one, usually Silverfeet, disdained the fangs of the other, hunched over the kill and gulped it down, hackles uprisen, lips peeled back in silent snarl, ready to dodge any attack that the loser might be disposed to deliver.

Early one afternoon the pups awoke, stretched, yawned, and looked to see what their parents were doing. The adult wolves dozed, content to let the pups amuse themselves alone. The pack had brought down a deer the night before and had fed well. The older wolves wanted to enjoy the contentment of a full belly and the pleasure of a lazy day. Not so the pups. They had slept several hours already, and although their bellies still bulged from last night's meal they were too full of energy to continue their sleep.

The two young wolves began to play, snarling in mock anger. The game took the young wolves away from the shelter of the balsams and down a short, slight slope into a small clearing. Here the two paused, panting, allowing their eyes to roam quickly around the natural glade. In another moment they were at it again, running and jumping and snapping, their mock growls loud in the afternoon stillness.

Suddenly Silverfeet, who was about to charge at his sister, stopped with raised head and sniffed at the new scent that had just reached him. In a moment he was off, his prancing gait telling the other pup that he was onto prey. She jumped to her feet and streaked after him, unwilling to let him enjoy this chase alone. Silverfeet ignored her. He ran faster, his nostrils guiding him unerringly towards a creature that the pups had not met before. Silverfeet had siphoned into his nose the odour of skunk.

The black and white, cat-sized creature was a young male who was out foraging for insects, carrion or anything else that was edible. He waddled slowly and uncaringly, secure in the noxious scent which the twin glands on either side of his anus were capable of discharging.

Startled by the sudden appearance of the two wolves, the skunk stopped, flinging his bushy, black and white tail into an upright position and peering shortsightedly at the brash beings who dared to invade his world.

Coming full tilt upon a small creature that did not immediately try to escape from them puzzled the wolves. They stopped their wild charge to take stock of the situation. Silverfeet whined, then yapped excitedly, jumping nervously in his frenzy. The quarry remained still.

Puzzled, the young wolves held back. The skunk used this pause to stamp his front feet. His warning was lost upon the inexperienced wolves. They did not know that this stamping preceded the discharge of the skunk's powerful spray.

Even as they watched, still hesitating, the black and white beast bent his body into the form of a U, head and tail facing his tormentors. From within the area of flared fur the retracted glands emerged smoothly, swivelled towards each other and became still, their nozzles set so that when the twin streams of musk were ejected by the skunk's powerful anal muscles, they would collide at a point some eight inches from where they emerged, to become a blinding, choking spray. The skunk waited, ready.

Silverfeet whined again, pranced lightly and made a sudden rush towards the skunk, mouth open and ears stiffly erect, the glint of hunting excitement filling his eyes. His sister copied his actions.

The skunk fired his salvo. The forward movement of both wolves was arrested instantly, as though a solid wall had become interposed between them and the skunk. Silverfeet, being closer, received the major share of the choking, stinging cloud, but his black sister was doused with enough of the acrid liquid to incapacitate her also.

Both wolves uttered shrill cries of anguish and surprise. They pawed at their muzzles and at their eyes and began rolling frenziedly on the ground, trying to suck air into their lungs in frantic gulps, but receiving, instead, further doses of the oily spray that still surrounded them. As they struggled with this new and horrible enemy, the skunk turned and ambled on its way, aware that it no longer had anything to fear from its attackers.

The powerful musk smell reached the adult wolves just as they were rising to investigate the disturbance. In another moment they flopped down onto the ground again, knowing that their young were not in danger and that they had learned yet another wilderness lesson.

By this time Silverfeet and his sister had recovered slightly from the shock and the power of the fumes. They moved away from the area where the musk was strongest and started rolling over the ground, pushing their faces against the soft mulch that covered the forest floor. The skunk spray was like acid in their eyes, burning and irritating; their throats were afire from the taste of it and the stench nauseated them. They were cowed and intimidated by this sudden, overpowering counter-attack from a small, furred creature that had appeared to be so harmless. Silverfeet and his sister would never forget this experience.

Four days later, just as they had recovered from their encounter with the skunk, the young black bitch met a porcupine for the first time. The pups were again seeking mischief while their parents dozed.

The night before had yielded five hares and one aging fox. Though the pack had fed but sparingly, the meagre rations of the night were enough to sustain them, at least during that day. But the pups had not yet learned that when hunting is poor, the hunter does not waste his energies during the hours of the day, when the pursuit of game is most difficult. So they ranged, while the adults rested in preparation for that night's hunting. They looked for prey, and found some small morsels: mice and a few bits of carrion. They played while they hunted, and this was another mistake, for when you hunt there is no time for distraction.

By their activity they made themselves more hungry. And because of their constant games they missed small creatures that otherwise they might have had. Then the black bitch smelled a new, yet faintly familiar smell. It came from a porcupine.

It was familiar because they had unknowingly been near a number of these creatures while hunting with their parents. But they had never seen one because the adults had always led them away from an animal that, if it could be counted on for a meal in the face of starvation, was yet too dangerous to chance when the living was easy.

Brash and inexperienced, the black bitch set her nostrils to the smell and darted away, leaving Silverfeet to investigate unopposed the tempting odour that clung to the crumbling edge of a groundhog burrow. While her brother was busy savouring and drooling, she burst through a clump of bushes and encountered the prickly black and yellow porcupine.

The wolf stopped suddenly, her hackles raised, the glint of sport in her eyes. The porcupine, caught by surprise, did not attempt to escape. Instead it placed itself in a defensive stance. Hunching its small head between stiffened forepaws, it raised its army of quills and turned its rump and club-like tail towards the intruder. It could do no more. When startled by such a powerful enemy it faced certain death if it tried to escape, hampered as it was by its clumsy, lumbering gait. It knew, did this creature of thorns, that its only hope of life lay in making use of the defences with which it had been equipped.

The young wolf anticipated a quick kill and a good feed, and she became impatient. She forgot the first lesson that the forest and her parents had taught; she forgot caution. Like a flash she charged the porcupine. As quickly the porcupine swivelled his body and met her charge with his bristle-stiff tail. As she leaned, open-mouthed, into the kill, the fearsome weapon lashed her muzzle.

In an instant the black bitch was convulsed. She yelped in agony and backed away from the porcupine, brushing frantically at the black and yellow barbs that filled her mouth and cheeks. As she struggled and howled, the slow, fat, clumsy porcupine waddled away, found a tall tree and climbed high into its branches, there to sit and peer down at its foe.

The young wolf was still brushing at the barbs in her face when Silverfeet reached her. He stopped, hackles raised and lips pulled back to reveal his fighting teeth, and took stock of the situation. His sensitive nose picked up the smell of the porcupine and quickly traced it to the quills in his sister's face. In another instant he located the porcupine in the tree and associated his sister's anguish with the strange, seemingly harmless creature that peered down at him. Through his sister's rashness Silverfeet had learned one more lesson. From now on he would link the porcupine with danger.

He turned to his sister, who had quieted, but who was still

trying to rid herself of the fearsome barbs, and he reached towards her with his muzzle. Baring his cutting teeth, he seized one quill and pulled on it, jerking his head sideways. The quill came out, leaving on the bitch's muzzle a droplet of scarlet.

By this time the parent wolves arrived. They, experienced, knew instantly what had happened, and soon the three were busy trying to remove the quills from the black pup. Although they were able to remove many of them, a number were out of reach inside the young wolf's mouth. Some, too, were cut by the teeth of the rescuers. Still, this rough and ready first aid was at least partly successful; it would allow the pup to eat, if painfully, and would assist nature in repairing the damage created by the barbs. Several days must pass before the painful throb in her mouth would subside, and for the next three or four weeks she would be marked by small festering lumps that would irritate constantly, until her iron constitution defeated the spear-like thorns.

Full in the cloudless sky a pale yellow moon beamed soft light on the wilderness. The heavens were crowded that night.

Against the moonlight the velvet dark glowed with the twinkling of a million stars, some flashing green, others giving off little bursts of ruby and orange, like diamond chips lying in a finger of sunlight. Now and then could be heard the whistle of fast-beating wings and the muffled voices of geese made restless by the pre-migration urge.

On a rock a lazy whip-poor-will chanted his dirge, more slowly now that his time was coming for the southward flight, not as monotonously as during the heat of summer. Sitting bolt upright on a pine branch a great horned owl boomed occasionally, his hoarse call echoing ghostly through the forest.

Grouped upon a bare outcrop of rock the four wolves sat still as statues, listening to the night. They were hungry and would soon set off on the hunt, but at that moment they seemed as though forced against their will to sit silent and immobile while the lesser things of the wilderness were allowed a few moments of peace. They squatted loosely on their haunches, heads held high, eyes focussed ahead, sharp ears erect. The big dog sat alone and to the right; the bitch was flanked on her left by Silverfeet, and on her right by her black daughter. Moonlight danced off their fangs and glistened on their guard hairs.

Half a mile from the wolves was a small lake. It was more of a pond, really — one of those untidy, marsh-bordered waterholes that dot the bushland, quenching the dryness around them and offering shelter to the water creatures. Downed trees tangled the shallow water in places, and tonight their stark arms were silhouetted against the reflection of the moon.

In the centre of the pond, discreetly surrounded by the sentinel shapes of cattails, stood a mound made of sticks and mud and decaying vegetation. Movement showed on top of the mound. A mallard stood there on one leg, preening his feathers slowly, occasionally uttering a short quack. Below the duck, within the darkness of his lodge, the old beaver was also grooming himself. Painstakingly, he was combing his belly fur, squatting like a ball upon his own tail, one back foot raised and cupped so that its long claws could be passed through the fur time and time again.

Last winter the beaver had not been alone. His mate and young had shared the lodge with him until, one by one, they had fallen to the steel gins set in the ice by the man who was now intent on trapping the wolves. The beaver had not mated again. He was too old to compete with the younger males that had prowled last spring in search of unattached females. He had tried, but he had lost his battles and had received more scars on his grizzled body.

Instinctively he knew that his time was growing short and he spent most of it within the safety of his lodge, going out only at night on short forays, eating quickly and returning to his lodge, swimming mostly on the surface, for his aging lungs would not allow him long periods under the water. He was doomed by age. He knew this, but he was trying to stretch just a little farther the thin thread of his life.

He finished combing his fur, paused for a moment and yawned: then he slid his tail out from under him and moved slowly towards one of the two holes that gave him entry and exit to the lodge. Clumsily he pushed himself into the aperture and entered the water, the valves inside his nostrils closing automatically as he became submerged.

For perhaps ten feet he paddled under the surface, then he rose. He steered upwards with his broad tail and as his head broke surface he snorted softly, opening his nose valves and clearing water from his nostrils. He paused, paddling. His eyes searched the shores. He listened. He began swimming slowly towards a canal that had been built by beavers, now long dead, to provide safe access to a heavy stand of poplars on the south side of the pond. Five yards from the canal mouth he paused again to listen and to look. Next he backed water and circled the area five times, swimming quietly, constantly seeking to detect the presence of his enemies. At last he was satisfied. He left the pond and swam up the canal until he reached the sloped, muddy landing place. Here he paused again and searched the dark forest before waddling up the short slope, towards a small tree that he had felled earlier that night. He began to feed, stripping the tender bark from the young, topmost branches, standing on his back legs and using his paddle tail as a prop.

Once he stopped, startled, and made to run back to the safety of the water as the rustle of dead leaves reached his small ears. But he was stopped by the churring voice of a raccoon and he resumed his feeding, stopping a moment to watch as the female raccoon and her five young ones rambled by, heading for the pond and the minnows they would find along its shores. Soon after this he was again interrupted, this time by a great horned owl which passed over him on silent wings as it searched the forest for prey. The beaver knew he had nothing to fear from the owl, and he continued eating.

On their rock the four wolves stirred. The dog looked at his mate, a quick flick of the yellow eyes containing a signal. In unison they rose and one by one bounded down, quick sleek shadows in the night. The bitch pulled into the lead, her mate just a step behind, the pups running in the rear. Once Silverfeet went to take the lead, but he was quelled by a swift look from his father. He dropped back. He knew the discipline of the hunt. He knew also that this was not the time for playfulness. Silently the pack ran.

Soon the wolves reached the environs of the beaver pond and the bitch slowed the pace. She had scented the beaver.

She turned and led the pack in a circle that would bring it downwind of the quarry. Just once, and very softly, she growled, turning her head towards Silverfeet, clearly telling him to keep position. The young wolf, eager and brash though he was, dared not disobey. He wanted to dash madly away, to short-cut towards the beaver, but training and instinct prevailed and he kept his place.

The she-wolf turned the pack . . . slowed . . . stopped. She looked at Silverfeet, who sat impatiently beside her. The young wolf immediately rose and went on alone, heading cautiously towards the sound and scent of the beaver. The bitch looked at her daughter and the young wolf knew that she must remain. This was to be Silverfeet's hunt. But the bitch did not fully trust her inexperienced son. She led the pack in another circle, running wide of the quarry, but intending to place herself in a position to intercept the beaver's frantic rush for the safety of the water should Silverfeet miss his attack.

In the moon-splashed forest Silverfeet padded softly, a powerful wraith intent on the kill. His mother need not have feared. The young wolf felt the urgency of this moment. He knew that this was his test; he sensed that after this kill he would occupy a position of equality in the pack. He inhaled the beaver scent deep into his lungs while his ears noted the eating noises made by the quarry.

Silverfeet stopped. He stood still, attuning his senses to the hunt. Only some fifteen yards separated him from the beaver. It continued eating, unaware that death lurked almost within striking distance. The horned owl hooted from somewhere nearby and the wolf allowed his eyes to swivel once towards the sound; then, he fixed his gaze on the spot where his nose and ears told him the beaver must be. In another instant he moved

forward, his body tense, his powerful muscles quivering, antici-
pating the call for action. He moved with infinite care, placing
each broad pad softly upon the ground, avoiding dry leaves and
brittle sticks that might crack or rustle and warn the beaver
before he could charge. He stopped again, gathering his
haunches for the leap. His entire body shivered slightly for an
instant. Then he launched himself.

The beaver turned away from the downed tree and twisted
his body, aiming towards the canal. But he was too late.

The wolf sprang at the fleeing beaver. He landed lightly after
his initial leap, bunched his legs and thrust himself into space
once more, coming down just two feet short of the beaver.

His reaching muzzle found the beaver's wet back, and his
fangs bit deep. The beaver screamed, once, and lashed his body
into a frenzy, desperately trying to shake the killing grip.

Silverfeet braced himself against the frantic struggles of his
prey. He shook his neck savagely to the right and opened his
jaws as the beaver fell sideways, exposing the underside of his
neck. Swiftly, Silverfeet bit into the beaver's throat, felt the
warmth of blood, tasted its salty tang. Then he went into a
frenzy. Growls formed deep in his throat and his eyes slitted as
he shook the dying beaver to the left and to the right. He shook
the beaver again and again, even after it was quite dead, and he
was still worrying the carcass when the rest of the pack arrived.
At once Silverfeet became transformed. He dropped the beaver, licked once at his bloodied lips, and growled, and this time
his voice contained a warning. He straddled his victim and
bared his fangs at his sister, telling her clearly that this was his
kill.

They stood quietly for a time, the parent wolves and the
black bitch forming a semi-circle around Silverfeet. Then the
old she-wolf moved forward and reached down, past her son's
bared fangs. She took hold of the dead beaver and dragged it
away from him. She dropped it, looked up at her son, and then
lay down beside the kill and began to eat. Seconds later the four
wolves had settled to the meal, and if Silverfeet growled now
and then between gulps, his voice held no threat. Rather there

was a note of pride in it. In ten minutes nothing remained of the beaver but a few pieces of fur and some chips of bone, scattered over the blood-stained ground.

Perhaps it was the success of his kill, or maybe it was the Indian summer night with its promise of winter to come, that acted on Silverfeet. Whatever it was, he suddenly rose to his feet, lifted his muzzle, and wailed his long, melancholy cry. The ululating song galvanized the others, and the forest night was suddenly filled with the deep baying of the wolves. At times their voices joined in chorus; at times they howled solo, one voice picking up where another left off. Howl after howl sailed upwards and over the trees, to float for a time in air and eventually become lost in an infinity of space. When it was over the forest was a place of stillness. Even the owls had hushed and it seemed as though the very wind had stilled its journey. Then the bark of a fox rang out, and the heart of the wilderness beat again.

The beaver had been but poor fare for the four wolves and they had need to hunt again this night, so, having finished their howl, they set off, aware that this would be a long hunt.

In his camp a mile south of the beaver pond the trapper heard the wolf howls. He was lying within the warmth of his sleeping bag idly watching the flickering spear of red that issued from his smoking fire. At once he sat up, looking towards the northwest, from where the sounds had come. A smile fixed itself on his thin lips.

He had been ranging that section of the forest for the past four days, looking for fresh sign of the wolves. During supper that night he had almost decided to abandon his quest; he was beginning to believe that the pack had left the area. He had hoped to strike a profit by either trapping or poisoning them, but they had so far eluded him, and recently he had failed even to cut their sign. Tonight he realized that they had headed farther north than he had thought.

Settling himself back in his bed, he decided to set out after them at daylight. He would first have to return to his home and load the livetrap onto his old truck, but he reasoned that the wolves would rendezvous during the daylight hours. This would give him enough time to reach that part of the forest where he guessed they would be sheltering.

With these thoughts he finally slept.

Unaware of man, the wolf pack trotted northwards in search of deer, the scent of which they had caught shortly after they had stopped howling. They ran abreast, strung out in a line, apparently without a definite plan of action.

Each wolf was busy with his own senses. Whether they were scenting the prey or listening for it would have been hard to tell from their actions; they carried their heads low, forming an arc from the tip of the nose up the neck, along the back and down the drooping tail. Sometimes one or the other would stop to investigate an attractive sight or smell, then turn back into the hunt, putting on a burst of speed to line up with the rest of the pack.

At one point their line of travel was blocked by a deep swamp. The pack split. Silverfeet cut around to the right of the obstacle; the rest went left. If there was strategy in this manoeuvre it was not apparent. Rather it seemed as though each member of the pack was busy with his own plans. Each wolf was equally excited by the fresh scent of deer, for their quarry had passed this way.

Silverfeet drew out of hearing of the pack and found himself travelling through low-lying, wet country, his passage made difficult by a succession of tangled deadfalls. He slowed. Once he hesitated and made as if to turn back; he could no longer scent the deer. But because the trail behind was as tangled as the route ahead, he kept going, following the contours of the swamp, stopping often to listen for sound of the others.

He travelled thus for some ten minutes; then, during one of his pauses, he heard rustling sounds. He knew at once that he had stumbled on deer, that the quarry was directly ahead. His ears and his nose told him that there were two of them, and that they had heard him and were turning back on their trail.

He redoubled his efforts, altering course away from the swamp, trying to keep the deer from escaping to higher ground. There was strategy in his actions now. He knew that by forcing them to the left, he would push them towards the rest of the pack.

His ruse worked. The deer had been turning away from the swamp, but hearing him on their right they altered course and followed the water's edge. Silverfeet, though tired, felt the urgency of the chase. Alone he would have given up, but the knowledge that the pack was somewhere ahead of the fleeing deer kept him at it. He put on a new burst of speed, and presently he caught glimpses of the tawny bodies as they fled in a desperate, outstretched gallop. Then he heard the pack. Seconds later he heard the thrashing of a downed body, and ran the harder.

When he reached the others they were already feeding on the carcass, and he took a place beside his father, panting, wet, muddy, and furiously hungry after the long chase. The big dog paused in the act of pulling meat off a rump to stare a fraction of time at his son and Silverfeet growled, perhaps in greeting, perhaps thinking that his father intended to bar him from the kill. But the dog turned again to the meat, and Silverfeet sank his teeth into the soft underbelly and ate ravenously.

For an hour they fed, at first greedily, slowly settling to a more leisurely pace as their hunger was appeased. Then they picked daintily, gnawing on bones, pausing to glance at their surroundings, now and then stopping to clean their muzzles and paws. At last they were sated.

Silverfeet rose, stretched and sauntered away, seeking a comfortable place upon which to lie and lick from his body the mud and wet that had coated it during the chase. One by one the others copied his actions until they were all bedded, clean, and composed for sleep within the thick tangle of deadfall and gnarled cedar where the kill had been made.

Dawn found them asleep. As the red sun climbed higher over the trees, it showed the remnants of the kill; it showed also the sleek black outline of another creature that was greedily eating.

The fisher had come soon after the wolves had finished their meal, but he had waited until now to risk his illicit feast, being well aware of the fate that would be his if, in his eagerness, he allowed one of the wolves to surprise him. He was an old hand at this sort of thievery, a quick black scoundrel the size of a fox, but shorter of limb, who dared almost anything for a meal and relied on his caution and speed to keep him out of trouble.

Once the she-wolf stirred in her sleep and the fisher froze, ready to bolt but not wishing to leave the feast until he was sure that his enemies were aware of his presence. When the wolf stayed quiet, the fisher bent once again to the deer's remains. He was still at it when three gray jays dropped from the sky and started to help themselves, squawking noisily at each other.

This was too much for the robber's nerves. He was sure the wolves would wake and catch him. Fixing his black shoe-button eyes on the jays, he attempted to scare them away, all the time knowing that these birds were even greater thieves than he was and could not be frightened by a mere glance. And so, unable to scare them away without waking the wolves, the fisher left on silent pads, leaving the birds to enjoy their meal.

It was full daylight; the sun was a flaming ball hovering over the forest. Birds called to each other, chickadees and tree sparrows and a host of others. In the marsh, ducks were paddling and calling. The high-pitched voices of geese came in clear as a great flock of Canadas flew low on their way to the beaver pond. The wolves were content. They woke occasionally, stretched, yawned, changed position, and went back to sleep.

The day held promise of autumnal warmth. A light wind plucked soft melody from the tree-tops, filching yellow leaves from the poplars. Somewhere on the beaver pond a bittern pumped his deep call, and a loon punctuated with ribald merriment the melodies of day.

It seemed that all was at peace, despite the gory remains of the deer. Night had been savage and full of death; day had dawned quiet, restful, and warm. But this was only an illusion. True, the big killers were at rest, but other hunters were busy in the forest.

In the shade of a rotting stump a shrew had just seized a white-footed mouse, sinking vicious little teeth into its victim's neck, its venomous saliva paralyzing the mouse.

A red-tailed hawk had struck, and now rose gripping the body of a chipmunk.

Under a canopy of browning ferns, a weasel was even then undulating towards a resting snowshoe hare. Too late the hare smelled the fetid odour of its enemy: it sought to flee, but was seized viciously by the neck. The weasel wrapped his sinewy body around his victim, biting deep, finding the jugular vein and hanging on, despite the frantic convulsions of the hare.

In the sky a questing shrike swooped with deadly efficiency on a fluffy chickadee, impaling the small bird with his sharp, down-curving beak.

Death and savagery were everywhere in the forest that day, as they are every day, no matter what the season, for this is the way of the wild; indeed, it is the way of life, which must have death in order to continue. The struggle is endless and assumes many forms: last night the powerful timber wolves; this morning all these other killers. Creatures must die so that other creatures may live. The old must perish and make way for the young. Last night the moon serenely watched the death struggle; now the sun beamed approval and the breeze murmured sanction.

6

The wolves awoke to the crashing of thunder. It came heralded by a flashing spear of light that dove spitefully at the earth, split, and roared its sullen anger. For a heartbeat the night forest was illuminated whitely, then the dark became intense while the crescendo of sound rumbled away into distance.

Came three more flashes of lightning; three drum rolls of thunder cascaded through the forest. The rain burst from belching clouds and fell in torrents, soaking the earth and the trees and the animals of the wilderness. This storm was the spearhead of winter. Gone was the softness of Indian summer. Full autumn had come, bringing with it the cold rains whose chill was just a fraction less penetrating than the kiss of frost.

Above the forest floor the trees shivered and cried their requiem to summer. Their leaves were torn from their branchlets and whirled into the vortex of the storm. Now and then some rotting branch would snap, the crash of its fall scarcely audible above the wailing of the wind and hammering of the rain. The animals and birds huddled in their bedding places and braced themselves against the storm, for there was no escape from its fury.

The wolf pack lay curled within the tangle of cedars, noses tucked into flanks and covered by their tails. They lay quietly, seemingly asleep, yet feeling the wet that soaked their bodies, feeling the misery of cold and the fearful shuddering of the earth when lightning smashed into it. But there was no fear in them. This was nature's might that they were exposed to; it was a natural thing, experienced in more or less degree many times before by the adults, who set the example for their young by accepting it, if not gladly, at least philosophically. So the pack rested, sometimes sleeping, then waking to lie unmoving. And towards dawn the rain stopped and the wind lost some of its violence.

The wolves, grateful for the respite, remained curled in their beds and slept. They were yet full of meat and would remain here until night came, and with it the need for more food.

A mile to the north, the trapper was busy as the rain let up. He had arrived in the area the night before, during the height of the storm, and had waited in his truck for the rain to cease. He was glad of the wet; it would wash off any vestiges of man-scent still clinging to the heavy-mesh wire cage that sat in the vehicle's cargo well. The cage was rusty; it had been left in the open, deliberately, because the trapper hoped in this way to keep his scent away from it. He had loaded it last night, slipping a cased rabbit skin over each hand while he arranged the trap, and he had been careful to place it on top of a deer hide that he had spread in the cargo well.

The man was a professional trapper. He knew the keen sense of smell of the animals upon which he preyed. And wolves, he knew, were the most suspicious of all wild creatures. Leave just a faint trace of human smell on the trap and they would avoid it. The storm would help to cover his traces.

When the rain stopped he was busy with snares, setting them in hare runways. He hoped that before long he would catch at least one to be used both for bait and for further masking his own scent on the trap. He set six snares and returned to his truck, to snatch some sleep while waiting for the hares to move after the storm.

He guessed that the wolves would stay in concealment during the remainder of this day, and he hoped that he had guessed right, for otherwise he would have to move on again in order to get ahead of his quarry. He had tracked them the day before, pinpointing their whereabouts to within a quarter of a mile of where they were now sleeping.

He thought he had plenty of time to catch a hare or two, unload the trap, and place it in position before dusk, when he would have to leave the area. With these thoughts, he composed himself for rest, curling up as best he could on the uncomfortable seat and tipping his wide-brimmed hat over his eyes. In five minutes he was snoring.

In the bush, life began to stir. Birds twittered as they searched for food; the red squirrels raced through the trees, now and then pausing in their quest for seeds and berries to chatter spitefully at one another.

The hares were moving. On the beaten trail upon which the trapper had set his snares a buck hare was hopping silently, stopping often to test for sounds and signs of an enemy. He was making his way to a patch of grass where he had fed the evening before. Always his long ears were on the move, searching out each sound, cataloguing it, dismissing it when it proved innocent. His life depended on his hearing and on his long legs, which could propel him speedily and in bounds of fifteen feet and more away from danger. But the threat that faced him now he had never encountered. It lay circular, cold and silent in his path, at times reflecting a thin sparkle of light: a cruel, strong wire waiting to choke the life out of him.

The hare stopped anew, swivelled his ears back and forth, and was satisfied. He bent his head to nibble at a tender young fern. He cut it from its stem and remained hunched while he ate it, his jaw moving from side to side. The uneaten portion of the plant protruded from his working mouth and slowly disappeared inside it. In a moment the fern was gone and the hare started forward again.

He was but inches from the snare now. As though sensing that something was wrong, he stopped again. But his questing ears could find no dangers in the forest around him and so, hesitant, still suspicious, he moved forward again.

At first he did not notice the noose. Its light touch was like the caress of a grass stem. But as he continued to move forward it tightened about his neck. He jerked his head to one side, trying to free himself, but the steel wire only tightened all the more. In an instant, panic filled the hare's mind.

With stiffened legs he jumped. The inexorable noose brought him crashing to the ground, tightening its hold still more. Again and again the hare sought to escape. He twisted violently from side to side, he bucked and pulled, his mouth agape, fighting for breath. His round brown eyes were bulging and glazed with terror and pain. But the steel wire held its grip.

The hare screamed, a shrill, piercing cry that echoed like some banshee wail through the morning forest. The voices of the day were stilled, as though the animals and birds were shocked into silence by the frenzied cry.

The wolves, too, heard the voice of the hare. They opened their eyes, listened, then went back to sleep.

The hare lay on his side, still kicking, but silent, needing to conserve his last breath. As he struggled, his mouth opened wide, his eyes seemed about to burst out of their sockets; there was a white froth at the corners of his lips. Weaker and weaker became his struggles, until at last, mercifully, his heart gave out. A shudder ran through the small brown body, the long back legs kicked once more, then the hare was still. The macabre dance of death was over.

The birds sang again, and some even went to look at the dead hare. Sitting in trees that overlooked the place, they stared down curiously, heads held sideways.

The man in the truck awoke, recognizing the scream. He yawned, stretched, rubbed his face with calloused, dirty hands, and smiled. One of his snares had found a victim. For a moment he debated whether to sleep some more, or whether to go and collect his prize. He still felt sleepy and was tempted. But the fear that one of the forest meat-eaters might find his hare, decided him. He yawned again and reached for a thermos of coffee. Unscrewing the plastic cup from its top he poured out some of the brew. When he had finished his coffee he screwed the cup back onto the flask and stepped out of the truck.

An hour later the man had unloaded his trap, baited it with the hare's body, and was back at the truck. He stopped beside the vehicle, his woodsman's eyes sweeping the forest. He climbed in behind the wheel, started the engine and reversed his way out of the area, content to let time have its way.

It was November, the last month of autumn. The air was made crisp by the previous night's rain. The hour was late evening. There was a yellow moon peering cold from a sky illuminated by the aurora; and there were stars, pale green and red and blue jewels studding a cloudless firmament. It was a wolf night, a night in which to run and cry wild.

Silverfeet was the first to stir, sitting up and yawning and doing the rest of his dog antics. One by one the others followed his lead. Silverfeet looked at the moon and wailed to it, and before the echo of his primitive solo had stilled over the forest the others gave tongue also. The wolf call rose clear and deep, first a medley, then quickly a solo as the wolves pointed their faces upwards and vented their emotions.

An owl joined them, a great gray owl. Its deep, repeated hoots, so different to the nostalgic call of the pack, yet blended into the song. It was thus for a time, the wolves and the owl and the gray dark of late evening, the moon and the pale stars. Then there was silence, an intense stillness, made palpable by the very contrast.

The pack was quiet, as though replenishing itself after the wild chant. One by one, led by the bitch, they rose and drilled their lean bodies into the lope, moving with that lithe grace that converts solid substance into fluid action. They sped into the darkened bush like wraiths, ghostly hunters ready to kill.

At first they ran in a straight line, heading directly for the place where the man had set his trap. But the bitch scented deer and she turned them, going towards the east, increasing her speed. The spoor was young and the pack was ravening.

Soon it was dark. This made no difference to the hunters, whose hearing and sense of smell were more than adequate for this kind of tracking. Already the wolves could hear their quarry and its scent was almost harsh in their nostrils, so strong was it.

The deer they were pursuing was old, a barren doe in whom the sickness of time had wrought its pitiless way. Age, the botfly maggots in her nose, and the parasites in her bowels had sentenced the doe. At the worst, she would die a slow, lingering death during the coming winter. At best, she would die quickly, her death meeting the need of the wolves. Still she ran, driven by the instinct of self-preservation and by fear of the hunting wolves.

But her stride was faltering. She inhaled through gaping mouth with harsh, rasping breaths, the sweat of exhaustion beading her cracked, black nose. She stumbled, and when she recovered she was facing in a new direction. She was heading towards the trap, which was almost two miles away.

Desperate because she knew that her pursuers were gaining, she took to a swampy area that was choked with downed timber and interwoven with thick clumps of alders. The place promised heavy going for hunters and quarry, but offered a little hope to the deer, whose long legs were more able to negotiate the jungle-like obstructions.

Through sluggish black water and springy, treacherous sphagnum the deer led the way, for a time keeping her lead, but slowly losing as her feeble reserves dwindled. The wolves charged through the swamp, leaping obstacles, splashing through the wet places, rushing heedlessly through tangles of dry branches.

The swamp thinned. It expired as the land took an uphill turn and sent the deer staggering up a slight slope into a growth of aspens.

At the top of this slope the wolves overtook her. The dog charged sideways into her backquarters, so that her legs tangled and she broke her stride and fell heavily to the ground. And before she could recover the old she-wolf sank flashing white teeth into her throat and Silverfeet bit deeply into one of her flanks. Pinioned by the two, the life blood already gushing from her wounds, the doe hardly felt the assaults of the dog and the black bitch.

The deer's soft eyes rolled upwards in her head. She gasped, shuddered, and was still. The wolves crouched to the kill and they fed.

Silverfeet wasn't hungry, but restlessness had him in its grip and he had left the others resting in the bedding place they had chosen the night before, after they had eaten their fill of the deer. The young wolf trotted slowly through the forest, stopping to listen and to smell, frequently leaving his sign at a scent station. He was rambling aimlessly, his senses attuned to the bush signs, yet not really hunting, for he had no need of meat; he was relaxed, curious, content to be alone on this quiet foray.

As he passed through an open glade the morning sun picked out the shine of his coat and brought into relief the sleek, powerful grace of his young body. It highlighted the fluid, stealthy ease of his movements. For an instant the sun picked him out, then he was gone, into the shadows of the trees.

He stopped under a tall pine and tested the smells of the forest. Something, a faint, tantalizing odour, had reached him. For perhaps twenty seconds he stood, head held high, nostrils quivering as he sniffed at the morning. He moved away at a gallop, his keen nose linking him to the source of the scent.

For five minutes he ran, then he stopped suddenly; a second scent had reached him.

Silverfeet sat down. He was puzzled. The first scent, strong in his nostrils, he recognized as coming from a hare. It told him that the hare was dead. But the other odour he had never come across before. While he was not afraid, the inbred caution of his race held him back. He could not identify the thing that was making the strange odour. It was not strong, but it was clearly noticeable and it came from the place where the hare was.

Despite himself he was drawn forward now that his nose had failed him. He could have turned away, and probably would have done so at another time, but his mood of restlessness made him curious. Had there been sounds for his ears to catch he might have been able to satisfy himself from a safe distance, but no alien sound came from the place ahead, of that he was sure.

A blend of inexperience and curiosity made him move ahead cautiously, shutting his mind to the warnings of his nature. Instinctively he knew he was breaking one of the rules of the wild, and just as surely he knew that the older members of the pack would have avoided the place, ignoring the tempting odour of new-dead hare for the safety of the familiar forest.

Soon he sensed that the object of his attention was near and he again stopped, allowing himself this much caution, but determined to investigate the strange thing and to taste it, if possible.

Standing with one forepaw raised, he listened for danger sounds. Only the known noises of the forest came to him as, in token caution, he sniffed the scents once more while his eyes strove to penetrate the thin barrier of foliage that separated him from the mysterious object. He stood poised for perhaps one minute, then he walked through the undergrowth. He was about to emerge from it when his eyes sighted the object of his interest. Instantly he froze. The cage stood where the hunter had placed it, deceptively quiet, seemingly innocent of evil. The two-inch wire mesh allowed Silverfeet to see the body of the hare lying on the floor of the trap.

Silverfeet was slightly alarmed, but still curiosity dominated his mind. He felt like sliding back into the forest; but the strange object did not move and the scent of the hare was enticing. His eyes were fixed unblinkingly on the trap, studying it. He was alert for the slightest sign of danger. For five minutes he stood staring and listening and smelling. Nothing happened. Slowly the feeling of alarm left him as the cage became more familiar with every passing instant.

He came out of concealment, stopped, stared again, and moved forward. Step by step, cautiously, his body rigid with tension, ready to fling itself into a fast leap to safety, he advanced.

He was but inches from the side of the trap and temptation prickled his taste buds. He inhaled the hare's odour and reached forward. His nose touched lightly against the cold wires of the trap, and in a flash he leaped back and prepared to run, still keeping his eyes on the cage.

Reassured by the inanimate character of the trap he advanced again upon it, this time moving more resolutely, and touching it with his nose immediately he reached it. Again he ducked away, but now he stopped, facing the trap, only two feet from it. His forward movement began again almost at once.

Deliberately he touched the mesh with his nose, and this time he did not shy away from the contact. He remained pressed against the side of the trap, like a child who flattens his nose against the window of a candy store. The drool ran from his mouth; in his mind he could already taste the hare. He pushed harder at the ungiving wire and when he could not part it as he would have done a bush, he sat on his haunches and puzzled over his problem. He could clearly see the hare's carcass and its scent was strong in his nostrils, but the unyielding mesh would not let him seize his prize. Presently he rose and began to walk around the trap, easing along its length, his head always turned so that he could watch the hare, and after making almost a full circuit in this fashion he came to the entrance.

Silverfeet stopped here. For no reason that he could understand he became tense now that nothing barred him from the hare. First he thrust his head into the square opening and held it there, stretching forward but not moving his feet. When nothing happened he took a tentative step with his right front leg, and paused. Nothing. He brought his left leg forward, shuffling his hind legs so that his head and shoulders were inside the trap.

He stopped and waited. There were no alarming signs. Then he could stand it no more. Quickly he ran forward, intending to grab the prize and escape, because he still did not fully trust this strange thing.

As his eager teeth grasped the coveted hare, there was a sharp, metallic click, followed by a loud crash.

Silverfeet had released the hare as soon as the first sound impinged on his mind. But it was too late. Even as he was turning, his body a blur of speed, the sliding door clanged shut. His bullet-fast body crashed jarringly against the heavy mesh.

Stunned by the jolt, he fell back, sprawling, legs kicking in the air. Already, blind fear had taken hold of his mind and with it came the instinctive curling back of his lips and the baring of his gleaming fangs. A low growl came from his throat. Then frenzy took hold of him. White foam spilled from his mouth; the yellow eyes were slitted, their pupils dilated. He snarled and snapped, and thrashed crazily about the cage. Again and again he flung himself at the relentless mesh.

He bit at the wire, gashing his lips and gums so that the blood flowed, and its sweet-salty taste drove him to more insanities. He snapped, growled, and whined, smashing his body into the unyielding steel of his prison. He was killing himself surely and unconsciously. The lithe, beautiful wild thing agog with the thirst of life, the hunting dog to which Creation had given such finely-strung powers of endurance and intellect, had in a trice disintegrated. In its place was a mindless thing, frantic, malevolent, tortured, bent upon its own destruction.

The trap did it. But the trap was only an instrument. It was the cruel, insensitive tool of man, the king beast — man, the dominant animal, whose body has degenerated while his brain has gained in size and powers. Not for man is the physical chase, the matching of muscle against muscle, the pitting of one sense against another until the hunted falls, or the hunter loses his prey. For him there must be easier ways to gain certain rewards while running no personal risk.

Man again triumphed that day. He had come and set his trap and a magnificent creature of the wild had fallen into it and become demented, lacerating himself against the cruel steel that he could not understand.

The pack was calling. Long and mournful its voice rose and fell as the three remaining wolves sought to bring back with their voices the one who had wandered away. The bitch and the dog and their black daughter called and called again, but no answering howl reached them.

It was early evening. The sun had slipped quietly out of the sky, seemingly chased into premature setting by the gray clouds that were drifting in from the northwest. Ahead of the clouds had come the chill of early winter and a kaleidoscope of sullen colours which forecast an autumnal storm. The fat, tumbling clouds were edged with rose and mauve, while here and there feeble fingers of sunlight played gently upon their undersides. On the forest floor a blue gloom tricked the eyes, making distant objects look near and near objects far away, and creating wraiths out of the wolves as they travelled silently through the evening.

The bitch was leading, her mate and her daughter trailing in her wake as she went towards the place where the trap had been set. Fear filled her mind. Instinct told her that Silverfeet would have answered the calls of the pack had he been able to do so. She knew that something had happened to him, but still she plodded onwards, unwilling to turn her back on him.

She stopped, sat on the ground, and howled again. At once the dog and the pup raised their muzzles and the three chanted their wail to the wilderness. For a while after this there was silence; the pack listened for a reply. None came. The pack moved again, and presently it reached the place where the trap had been set.

The entangled scents of man, wolf, hare and steel confused

and frightened the wolves. Of a sudden the black pup bolted, streaking away to the north, instantly followed by the bitch and her mate. The three wolves fled as though pursued by demons, all thoughts of Silverfeet banished now from their minds. The dreaded smell of man spurred them away from that place.

Silverfeet was many miles away from where he had been trapped, his steel prison bouncing and rocking in the back of the hunter's truck. The clangour that it made against the metal of the truck swelled the volume of terror that had seized his mind. His imprisonment, the cruel buffeting of the cage, and the sight and smell of man had combined to rob him of sanity.

The captive bore little resemblance to the handsome wolf of but a few hours ago. Blood flowed from the cuts on his lips and gums, staining his neck and chest. His front paws were torn and bloody, their claws ripped off during his futile battle with the steel cage. As he lay crumpled and broken in the bottom of the trap, his eyes were dead things. The hair on his body, which earlier that day had reflected the sunlight, was dull and matted, worn away in places by his frantic struggles to escape.

He had been savagely fighting the cage when the man had come earlier that evening. Lost in fear and wild struggling, he had realized the man's presence only when he was standing a couple of paces from the trap, a satisfied smile on his thin lips.

For an instant the wolf and the man stared at each other, and in those brief time-ticks was born an undying hatred. The wolf instantly stilled his frantic scrambling and crouched on the cage floor, his yellow eyes meeting the gaze of his captor with such a blaze of fury that the man shifted uneasily.

The man felt fear, even though the wolf was held by the cage. And because the captive, despite his helplessness, had been able to make the man uneasy, the trapper became ashamed of his emotions, instantly denying them to his conscious being, forcing them back into the deep places of his mind. To banish his fear the man conjured up hate for the wolf. He could have achieved his purpose more easily with compassion. But he was not a compassionate man. He chose hate.

Still avoiding the fury that blazed from those eyes, the man muttered to himself, hesitated, then looked around, searching for a stick. He found one; a dead pine branch with a jagged point. He strode to it, picked it up and returned to the cage. Keeping his distance, he pushed the thin, pointed end through the mesh to poke cruelly at the wolf's face.

Silverfeet backed away from the stick, twisting his body, retreating against the far wall of the cage only to swing back fast and snap at the object that seemed to him to be an extension of the hated being who stood leering outside the cage. From his throat emerged a deep, savage growl. There was a flash of bloodied fangs. The stick snapped and the man, unnerved by the attack, jumped back, letting go of the pine branch.

The man cursed loudly. His voice held mingled fear and hate. Again the beast had brought humiliation to him. It was unforgivable. Man was the master of all things. He was the king beast. It was unthinkable that a caged wolf could instill raw fear in such a superior intellect. Ashamed, but aware that the memory of this day would linger, the man again sought to banish his fear with hatred. He darted forward, picked up the stick and smashed again and again at the cage, cursing the wolf. And when he stopped, the stick in his hand broken short, he was sweating with fury.

No such complications existed in the simple mind of the wolf. He knew fear; rank, bitter-tasting panic that forced the juices from his gut. He knew hatred; wild, blazing hatred for the man, for the gangling, flailing sight of him, for the sour smell of him, for his cruel voice. The wolf accepted his fear and was not ashamed of it. He accepted his hate and had no power to prevent it. He stayed crouched, alert for another attack, as he kept his eyes glued to his captor. He lay there bloody, shaking, fearing, hating, his belly shrunken into his flanks, his tail tucked tightly against his loins. His lips parted in a silent snarl, revealing the gleaming, red-stained canines; and with every fibre of his being he longed to sink his fangs into the man's soft throat and tear the life from him.

7

The memory of those hated, fearful moments when he was face to face with his enemy still lingered in the wolf's mind, mingling with the new terror that came with each jolt as the cage bumped and bounced in the truck bed.

But nature was beginning to aid Silverfeet, dulling his mind, triggering within his body those mysterious reactions that come, sooner or later, to the wild thing that finds itself suddenly caged and surrounded by the fearful contact of man. He lay huddled on the cage floor, his body flaccid except when it was gripped fleetingly by the sharp, nervous quivering that accompanies shock. Instinctively he braced himself against the buffeting of the truck. Now and then he licked his bloody lips. Once, when gripped by nervous tremor, he voided his bowels and bladder, unable to stop himself, feeling the warm spread of his urine and feces as they combined to further humiliate him. He vomited. Eventually he lay spent, his eyes closed, his breathing slow. He was resigned, for the time being, to the horror that engulfed him. He lay like that for almost two hours, and then the truck squealed to a jarring halt, throwing him violently against the rear of the cage.

Silverfeet backed to the centre of the trap, eyes open again, lips peeled back. His heart was a wild thing inside his breast, a run-away pump trying to force its way out of his body. He crouched, fearful, in deep shock, sick at heart. But he was not subdued. The indomitable spirit of the wild persisted and gave him the will to face his enemy, to defend himself as best he could; to die if he had to, but to die fighting. He crouched and he waited.

The sound of the truck door opening merely caused him to bunch his muscles as he arranged himself for a spring. The slamming of the door as the trapper got out of the truck stirred within his brain a vortex of emotions, threatening to rob him of sanity. But, somehow, he hung on and waited as the heavy footsteps of the trapper approached the tailgate of the truck.

Wolf and man stared at one another again. And once more the hate in the yellow eyes of the wolf caused the man to flinch involuntarily. For perhaps ten seconds they stood thus; the man with one hand on the tailgate, the trapped wolf crouching, his gaze fixed upon the man's face. Then the trapper laughed, seeking to cover his fear. With an air of bravado he unsnapped the hooks that held the tailgate in place and let the heavy metal drop down with a resounding clang. To his surprise, Silverfeet did not flinch at the sudden noise. The wolf remained crouched, showing his teeth. His eyes remained fixed on the man.

From the truck box the trapper took the two iron hooks with which he had lifted the cage into the truck. He fastened one on each side of the cage, steeling himself against any possible lunge by the wolf when his hands came near the wire.

Silverfeet had risen. He remained standing in the cage, his

eyes moving from side to side, all his attention centred on the hooks and on the man's hands. By now he knew that his tormentor was safe while he stood on the other side of the wire barrier. He wasted no more energy in futile charges. With the patience that all wild things can muster, he waited, biding his time, still hoping to get free of the trap and to spring for the throat of the trapper. He no longer had any fear of the man, only hatred. The wolf's fear was for his imprisonment; for the mesh walls of his cage, for the noises it made as it was dragged towards the end of the truck.

Presently half the cage was overhanging beyond the dropped tailgate. It balanced there for a moment while the trapper made sure that the catches held the sliding door securely. With a thin-lipped grin twisting his face, the trapper deftly released both hooks simultaneously and let the cage fall to the ground.

The toppling cage propelled Silverfeet upside down against the cage roof. The wolf scrambled madly to keep his balance but his efforts were useless. The cage hit the ground with a jar that sent him crashing into one side, his head hitting the wire. His body somersaulted, so that for an instant his entire weight pressed downwards on his neck. The force with which his head struck the cage stunned the wolf; the sudden pressure on his bent neck almost broke his spine. Through a dim haze he felt the pain. The cage settled on its side and was still. Silverfeet lay inert, panting. He was helpless for the moment, and his helplessness brought pleasure to his captor.

"That'll teach you, varmint!" the man said loudly, as he again fastened the hooks in the mesh and began dragging the cage towards the ramshackle, clapboard house that was his home.

Bringing the cage to a stop beside the door of the house, the man released the hooks, stood back, and gazed speculatively at his captive. He nodded to himself, having arrived at a decision. He returned to the truck, closed the tailgate and went back to the house.

As he passed the cage he gave it a kick that sent it rocking again and he laughed loudly as Silverfeet sought frantically to retain his footing. With his hand on the handle of the house door, the trapper turned for one more look at the wolf.

"Mebbe a night in that cage'll cool you off, varmint," he said. And he turned and entered the house.

The man's name was Morgan. He had a first name, but few people knew it and it was said that he did not remember it himself. To his face his neighbours referred to him as Morg; behind his back they called him other names, for though his services were needed by the farmers and ranchers of the area, who now and then lost stock to coyotes and foxes and paid him to get rid of the raiders, he was not a man who inspired liking. His calling dictated that he live a solitary life, and because his living depended upon the killing of animals he had become coarsened, unfeeling. He was not deliberately brutal or cruel; he simply had no feelings for the wild things that he hunted. A hare strangled in a set represented merely food and a few cents for the pelt that he jerked from its body; a muskrat mangled in a trap held value only as a pelt. A beaver was a big prize; it offered dollars in exchange for the tedious task of skinning, and the added reward of musk scent which he used to attract other creatures to his traps.

So Morgan lived alone in the frame house that was steeped with the smells of decay. He lived with skins tacked to his walls, placed there to dry. He lived with himself; he had few friends and he felt contempt for the men who sought his services. He knew their feelings for him; he knew their distaste for his calling. But deep within him was an instinctive scorn for the men who would pay him to be their executioner yet who would not willingly undertake the job themselves.

So Morgan lived alone. He followed his trapline and he killed and he skinned, and any pity that he might once have felt had left him. Solitary and coarse, he followed the only trade he knew, content if the trapping was good, angry if the coveted creatures managed to elude his traps.

That night he lit his fire, cooked his supper and stretched out on his bed without a thought for the trapped wolf that lay, apathetic and suffering, outside his door. And Morgan slept, snoring loudly.

Silverfeet was awake, but his senses were dulled. At first he had squatted in his small prison, listening to the noises of the man inside the house. His nose continued to sense the odours that surrounded him. There were many smells, some familiar, others strange and frightening. One smell dominated all — the smell of his captor, an odious, sickening aroma that, while it no longer held fear, aroused a thirst for killing such as Silverfeet had never experienced before.

To the wolf, time seemed endless. He was hungry, he was dirty and cramped, his body hurt, and so, like his mother when she had faced starvation alone and had sought solace in sleep, Silverfeet closed his consciousness to his plight. At first he merely dozed, lifting his head often as some new sound or smell reached his dulled senses. Once he raised himself to his haunches and launched his lonely, melancholy howl into the night.

At last he sank down, curled himself into a tight ball, closed his eyes, and slipped into a sleep that was more coma than slumber.

The moon came up. It hung full, round, and lemon yellow in the sky, bathing with its light the semi-conscious wolf. It seemed to be comforting him, telling him that from its great height it could offer a link with the wild pack, for its rays penetrated the entire forest. An owl pounced on a mouse and the rodent's shrill, short scream voiced the protest of life as it was forced to give way to death. Still the wolf remained huddled in his cage.

Once a shrew was drawn to the trap by the smell of the wolf's blood. It eased its little, blue-gray body through one of the squares of mesh and was almost upon the wolf before its senses signalled that life yet remained in the captive. With a soft squeal it vented its fear and frustration as it scuttled swiftly away. If Silverfeet noticed he gave no sign.

He lay immobile. His nose was buried in his flank, his breathing was lethargic. Occasionally raw nerves caused his skin to undulate in fast, pulsing waves; now and then a slight shudder would convulse his body for an instant. But none of these things reached the tortured mind that had taken refuge in trance.

The night grew older. The moon weakened. Somewhere in the distance a rooster crowed defiance and the owl hooted an answer as it glided silently towards its daytime perch in the rafters of a tumbledown building.

One by one the stars paled. The blue-black of night sky turned to sea green, lightened still further, then took on a tinge of rose as the sun inched upwards towards the rim of the land. Silverfeet remained curled up, secure in his mental vacuum, alive yet unaware. He was a creature lost, despondent, distraught. He was the spirit of the wild destroyed by the thoughtless and uncaring hand of man.

That was how Morgan found him when he emerged from his house later that morning. The man opened his door, paused in its frame and yawned, scratching his shirt-clad torso. He closed his mouth, dropped his arms, and looked at the cage. His black eyebrows rose in surprise at seeing the uncaring wolf. Then he frowned. He was disturbed by the wolf's apathy, by the absence of that ferocious spirit that had frightened him the previous day. But he felt no pity for the wolf. His concern was for the profit that he hoped to realize from the live animal. Slowly he approached the cage. He stopped, bent to look more carefully at the wolf and straightened again, still frowning.

Tentatively Morgan kicked the cage, a soft, nudging kick that merely rocked it slightly, to see if the wolf responded to the disturbance. Silverfeet moved his head a little and opened his eyes. Beyond that, nothing. The eyes were dull, uncaring, and the body remained still. Morgan cursed, then retraced his steps to the house. Presently he emerged carrying a small piece of raw meat. Carefully, using a stick, he poked this through the mesh and let it fall a few inches in front of Silverfeet's nose. The wolf ignored it. His eyes closed again and he thrust his head deeper into his flank. Again Morgan cursed.

His problem was simple. If the wolf died, he would get

nothing for his efforts. Bounties on predators had long been removed and Silverfeet's coat would bring nothing on the fur market, dry and matted and bare in patches as it was. And Morgan knew that no zoo would pay for the live wolf in its present state. He pondered, standing by the cage and watching the captive, trying to find a solution to the problem.

Finally he nodded to himself. He had decided. He would have to keep the wolf on the premises until it either recovered or died. He hoped it would recover if he put it in larger quarters and left it alone for a time, showing himself only to give it food and water. But where to house it? He had no suitable pen and construction of a proper enclosure would take time and cost money. He did not want to go to so much trouble over a creature that represented profit only if there was a minimum of work involved. Then he remembered the old henhouse. It was built of logs, and had a metal roof and one small window. This would do, if he nailed wire mesh over the glass and cut a small, square hole in the bottom of the door through which he could put in meat and water. With that he went to work, and an hour later he had finished the job. He felt pleased. He was hopeful that the wolf would slowly recover.

Going back to the cage he found that Silverfeet had not moved. This pleased him now, for it would be easier to put the wolf into the henhouse if it remained docile.

With the hooks he dragged the cage to the henhouse, opened the door of the building and lifted the cage over the low step, pushing it with his foot and making sure that the sliding door of the cage faced the door of the new prison. At this point he puzzled over the need to release the wolf from the trap without being attacked by it or allowing it to escape, but eventually he solved this problem also. With a brace and bit he drilled a small hole in the door, near its top. Then he found a brass cuphook and screwed this into the roof of the building immediately above the door of the cage. He found some twine, threaded it through the hole he had drilled in the door, passed it through the hook in the roof and then tied it to the top of the sliding door of the trap. He released the door's catches.

Silverfeet watched his captor during all this, but he showed little interest and none of the savagery with which he had greeted the man on previous occasions. Morgan looked at the wolf for a moment, then went out of the building and closed the door, securing it with a stout catch.

He grasped the string and pulled, and the sliding door of the cage eased upwards. When it was fully opened, Morgan tied the string to a nail and stooped to look through the hole that he had cut in the henhouse door. A smile creased his lips. Silverfeet was showing more interest. He had lifted his head and was eyeing the opened door of his prison. Morgan left, going to the house in search of a pan for water and some more meat.

When he returned, Silverfeet was standing in the cage with his head outside the opening. But still he looked listless. Morgan threw the meat into the cage; with a stick he pushed the pan of water just inside the small trapdoor; and he left.

The henhouse was a small structure, twelve feet square, that had been unoccupied by anything, save perhaps a few mice, for many years and had not been cleaned out since the last chicken was removed from it. Though its log walls were solid, they were badly chinked with lime mortar; and this was fortunate, for through the cracks a few rays of light and a little fresh air reached the gloomy interior. The one small window, grimed and covered now with wire, served only to admit a little diffused light. The floor was cement, but this was visible in only a few places, for the old litter, decomposed into a sour-smelling mulch, covered most of it. This building offered the captive but one small advantage over the trap — more space.

Silverfeet remained standing inside the wire cage for almost half an hour after Morgan went away. He wanted to leave the confines of the trap, but he was suspicious of this new place; his instincts forced him to check out every nook and cranny before he ventured into it. But as his mind began to function more normally, he became conscious of hunger and, particularly, of thirst. His nose told him that food and water stood near the door; and he dared a little more and thrust his neck and chest out into the gloom. Confidence slowly returned to him now that he was alone, and at last he stepped onto the litter of the henhouse floor.

This action, small as it was, further awakened his dulled mind. He instantly became wary, and stood with feet and legs bunched, ready for immediate action. But when nothing happened, and as he became accustomed to the sights and smells of the place, he relaxed a little. He was certainly not his normal self, but at least most of his keen intellect had returned and the urge for self-preservation began to course through him once again.

Moments later he walked stiff-legged towards the door and the container of water. He stopped a couple of paces from it and smelled it. He immediately detected the odour of his enemy, and he curled his lips in a silent threat. He stood bristling before the metal pan, debating whether or not to charge at it, for it was heavy with Morgan's scent. In the end his intellect won out. He realized that, though connected in some way with the man, the water pot offered no threat. He went to it and drank thirstily, not stopping until it was empty.

The meat attracted him and he put his nose to it, but again he encountered Morgan's smell. He stood over it for some moments and the drool came into his mouth. But the meat was tainted by his enemy. He walked away from it.

He prowled, exploring every inch of his new prison. Instinct urged him to escape from it, and such was the urgency of his desires that he forced his crippled feet to endure the pain of walking. Once he tried to scratch at the small trapdoor that Morgan had cut, but he whimpered with pain when his raw toes encountered the rough wood. An hour later he gave up and slumped despairingly in the darkest corner of the henhouse, lying on his side, licking his lacerated front paws. Then he slept. And he had a dream.

Freedom came to his sleeping mind. Once more he was free to course with the pack that was running a deer. The chase was hot. The snow was deep and crusted and the wolves could run on top of the hard surface, while the deer's sharp hoofs cut through it. The prey was floundering and exhausted, and the pack was closing for the kill. The sleeping wolf whined his eagerness as in his dream he spurted forward to place himself alongside his quarry and readied himself for the lunge that would cause the deer to break stride and fall. In his sleep Silverfeet's legs were moving, twitching at first, then pumping intermittently. It was this that woke him.

Such was the reality of the dream that at first he could not understand his surroundings and he quickly rose to his feet. Memory returned. With it came the terror of captivity and the hate for the man, and he vented his feelings in the only way that he knew. Squatting in the filth of the henhouse he raised his broad head and howled his sadness.

Morgan heard the sound and was pleased. He reasoned that if the wolf could howl there could be little wrong with him. He had been preparing some traps that he intended setting out the next day, but the howls drew him to the henhouse. He unfastened the trapdoor and bent to peer inside.

Without warning, a growling, snapping fury thrust at him. Such was the speed of the wolf's attack that the sharp canines reached the index finger on Morgan's left hand and laid it open to the bone. Morgan cursed and slammed the trap shut and backed away from the henhouse, fear pumping his heart and convulsing his bowels. He clutched at his mutilated finger and the sight of the spurting blood put more fear into him. He turned and ran for the house and there he dressed his wound, his face pale, his mouth contorted by the rage that came to replace his fear.

When he had bandaged his wound he stood in the centre of his kitchen and looked at the rifles that hung on pegs on one wall. He strode to the weapons and took one of them down, then went to a table and rummaged among the oddments that cluttered it until he found a box of shells. He loaded the rifle.

Greed won in the end. Its voice reached him as he was striding to the door, the loaded gun clutched in his good hand. He stopped, and Silverfeet's life was spared. Shooting the wolf, Morgan knew, would bring him no profit, only the job of towing the carcass to the pit where he disposed of what remained of the hapless creatures he trapped, after he had removed their pelts, and leaving it there for scavengers. He knew that the wolf's pelt was worthless after the abuse that it had taken. This stopped him. He unloaded the gun and returned it to its place on the wall. But all the time the pain in his finger fanned his hate, and his rage increased when he realized that he was at the moment powerless to take his revenge upon the wolf. Consternation changed the set of his countenance.

Realizing that he could not get at the wolf without shooting it, he became aware of the predicament that would be his when Silverfeet recovered and must be returned to the cage for shipment to the zoo. He had not stopped to think about this problem when he had turned the wolf loose in the henhouse. Now, it wiped hate and rage from his mind and furrowed his brow as he tried to find a solution. He could not open the door of the henhouse and seize the wolf, that was obvious. The beast was too dangerous to face.

Morgan cursed the wolf again. He was beginning to wish that he had not gone to all the trouble of capturing it alive. Had he set out poison, he thought, he might have got two or three wolves and their prime hides would have been worth quite a few dollars. As it was, the pack had left the area, and here he was with a live wolf on his hands whose pelt was worthless and which he could not remove alive from the henhouse. Or so it seemed.

Morgan found a bottle of whiskey and a glass and poured himself a stiff drink. Nursing his finger, he sipped the whiskey and thought about his latest problem.

In the henhouse Silverfeet paced back and forth with renewed vigour. Once more his eyes glowed with fierce wild light. The taste of the man's blood had done that for him. Once again his keen brain was fully alive. Urged by hunger, he had eaten the meat that Morgan had left, willing to face the smell of man now that he had tasted human blood.

He stopped suddenly, facing the window. He looked at it for some moments, then backed as far away from it as his confinement would allow. He crouched an instant, then launched himself forward, hitting the screen wire with such force that, although it held his weight, it was pushed outwards and his stiff paws smashed the glass.

He recovered his balance in mid-air, and landed lightly on the floor. There he paused fractionally before backing to the far wall in preparation for a fresh leap. But first he licked his right paw; the glass had inflicted a cut. Morgan, who had heard the smashing of the glass, appeared outside the window just as Silverfeet launched himself again.

The wolf was already in mid-air when he saw the man. His lips peeled back, his growl was low but charged with hate. The man saw the fearsome, gaping mouth of the wolf coming straight for him, the blood which Silverfeet had licked from his paw staining the jaws crimson. It was a horrifying sight.

Morgan ducked in sudden panic, expecting the furious wolf to land on top of him. The wire held, though it creaked in protest and bulged out a little more. Pieces of shattered glass fell on top of Morgan and one of them cut his neck slightly so that blood flowed. Silverfeet smelled the blood. It drove him to frenzy. He charged at the wire again, still growling, his jaws working in his eagerness to get at the man.

But Morgan was no longer there. He was running for the house, fearful, continually glancing over his shoulder, his face ashen, the blood from the slight cut running slowly down his neck and over his chest, increasing his panic. He slammed the door of his house when he reached it, and then leaned against it as though expecting the wolf to come charging after him.

Silverfeet hit the wire once more. Again it bulged out. Some of the staples that held it in place released their grip, and two small gaps appeared between the window frame and the wire. Had the wolf charged two or three times more he would have found his freedom. But he stopped. The man had gone and Silverfeet was spent. His front paws, mutilated by the loss of his claws, throbbed agonies that dulled his mind, and the cut inflicted by the glass was bleeding profusely. The wolf lay down and licked his hurts.

In the house Morgan had recovered somewhat from his fear. He again held a loaded rifle; he also held a hammer and had thrust some nails into his mouth. Carefully he opened the door and peered out, the rifle ready; but outside there was no danger.

Walking softly, Morgan went around to the back of the house. There he found a square of plywood large enough to fit over the window. He thrust the hammer in the back pocket of his levis and gripped the wood clumsily with his injured left hand. Holding the gun in his right, fully cocked and ready to fire, he walked towards the henhouse, fear in his heart, but greed dominating his mind. He was sure that the wolf would recover and would fetch a good price at the zoo. But he was not sure that it was still in the henhouse. He knew that the wire over the window could not withstand many more of the infuriated animal's lunges. He hoped that he was still in time.

Slowly he approached the henhouse. Beside its door he stopped and listened. Above the beating of his heart, he heard faint movement inside the building. Silverfeet had heard him coming and had stood up. Morgan moved carefully to the corner of the building, from where he could see the window. There he paused again. All was quiet. Placing the rifle against the building, he put both hands to the plywood and, holding it before him like a shield, he ran to the window and slapped the wood against it, holding it there with his weight. Instantly the wolf charged and the wood was almost knocked out of Morgan's grasp. But it held.

Quickly, knowing that the wolf would soon leap at the window again, Morgan slipped a nail out of his mouth, and grabbed the hammer from his back pocket. Pushing against the wood with his left hand, he started the nail home with three strong blows. At this moment Silverfeet charged and the plywood bounced under Morgan's hand; but again it held, and the man finished driving the first nail.

Perhaps it was the noise of the hammer that made Silverfeet hesitate. By the time he jumped at the window again, Morgan had banged home his second nail and the wood held against the lunge. Quickly Morgan finished nailing the wood in place, making sure, putting a line of nails all around it. Then he went in search of larger nails and two pieces of two-by-four lumber. These he fastened against the plywood and when he was done he felt sure that the wolf would not be able to escape.

Silverfeet charged again, but this time the solid wooden barrier threw him backwards and he crashed heavily on the cement floor, hurting his spine. Whimpering, his spirit cowed, he limped to a corner and lay down.

Once more his mind saved him, taking him into the twilight zone that borders on coma, and he stayed thus for two days, ignoring the man when he came with meat and water. And Morgan worried once more.

On the second day, thirst drove Silverfeet to seek water. Painfully he uncurled himself and stood up, so weak that he could hardly keep his balance. He hobbled across his dark prison towards the water pot and drank, finishing all it contained. With his nose he pushed at a piece of half-rotten meat, but he spurned it, walked back to his corner, and settled down again. But now that he was awake, his mind came out of hiding, and he set about trying to ease his sore body. His toes had scabbed over, and the cut on his pad was healing, but he licked them clean. For his spine he could do nothing. It was bruised where it had hit the cement, but that would pass.

When he had finished licking his wounds he rose again, the pangs of hunger forcing him to go back to the meat that Morgan had tossed in. There were three pieces, in all perhaps two pounds of fetid beef. Silverfeet gulped it down. Then he nuzzled the water pot again, but it was empty. So he went to his corner, lay down, and slept. It was a true sleep this time, marked by dreams, but refreshing, the kind of sleep that would allow his body to recuperate some of its lost strength. Once during the night he was awakened by a scurrying mouse. He pounced at it, but he was still too weak and the mouse got away.

The next morning Morgan was elated to find the meat gone and the water pot empty. He fished out the pot gingerly with a stick, and took it back to the house. There he replenished the water, and from the carcass of a deer that he had killed the previous day, he cut off a generous portion of meat. Back at the henhouse he opened the trapdoor and stood back, waiting for the wolf to charge. But Silverfeet was learning the rules of captivity. By now he knew that the opening of the trapdoor meant food and drink, so, though he still longed to sink his fangs into the man's throat, he held himself back, some instinct telling him that if he were ever to escape he must first build up his strength.

When the door closed he went to the food. He ate and then he drank, and although the meal was meagre it gave him strength. But his new-found energy, weak though it was, increased his longing to be free again, to run wild, to find his pack, and to bed with them in some cloistered hollow in the forest. He wanted to howl free once more, to range the forest in search of prey, to take his chances with the hard life of the wild wolf. But he could not have these things and so he lay down to sleep, to seek forgetfulness.

The spark of life dies hard in all things. Small and feeble though it may be at times, it has yet the power to keep death at bay, to struggle against the impossible, sustaining itself with occasional fragments of hope. Silverfeet wanted to live, and he did battle with a part of him that said: "Die, wolf, die, in this dark, sour prison."

As one day followed another the wolf ate his allotted ration of meat and drank his pan of water. Never was there enough meat to round his belly, nor enough water to fully slake his thirst. Once every morning Morgan opened the trapdoor, threw in the meat, hooked out the water pot, replenished it, and pushed it back in with a pole. He was very careful, now, to keep his hands out of reach of the wolf's fangs. And Silverfeet was always there, ready, hopeful that when the square of daylight became visible it might somehow offer freedom.

At the end of ten days Silverfeet's injuries were almost fully healed and he had regained some more of his lost strength. He was thin, his coat was still dull and brittle and rubbed away in places, and he reeked of rotten hen manure, of the mulchy dampness of the place, and of the odour of his own excrement, which, in his efforts to maintain himself clean, he always deposited in the same corner of the henhouse. He walked more surely, though he still favoured his front paws, the nails of which had not yet grown back.

Daily Morgan peered through the trapdoor in an attempt to note the wolf's condition, and every time his face came level with Silverfeet's eyes, the wolf's savage growl made him straighten hurriedly. Then, at the end of two weeks, Morgan came with another man. The two stood outside the henhouse talking. Their words meant nothing to Silverfeet, but their voices fanned his smouldering hate for all mankind. He had been curled up in his bed corner when he heard them. Instantly he arose and padded over to the trapdoor, standing squarely before it, head down, his teeth bared. But he did not utter a sound.

"He's not in bad shape now," Morgan was saying. "Mebbe a bit thin but he'll do, especially after a few weeks in a proper cage."

"Well . . . a hundred dollars is high for a wolf," the second man said. He was of medium height, and fair. He spoke softly.

Morgan frowned, scratched his head and looked into the distance.

"Listen, you don't know the trouble I had with that varmint. Even got my finger bit, right down to the bone. He's worth a hundred."

"No, not to me, he isn't. Tell you what. I'll give you seventy bucks, and that's it. And not till after I've seen him."

Morgan continued his study of the horizon. He wanted the money, but now, perversely, he did not really want to sell the wolf. Silverfeet had become to him a symbol of power. He still feared the wolf, but unconsciously he was glorying in his hate for him, taking personal satisfaction in keeping him a helpless prisoner. Greed and hate jostled each other in his mind. But greed won.

"O.K.," he said, finally. "You can have him for seventy an'

be damned to the varmint. He's caused me enough trouble already."

The zoo man carried a flashlight. He had it ready in his hand as he squatted to see into the henhouse. He told Morgan to open the trapdoor.

"Watch yourself now," Morgan warned. "That wolf's a killer!"

He opened the trapdoor. A growl and the snapping of teeth greeted the men. Silverfeet's muzzle thrust itself through the square, the lips curled back, the jaws working, seeking a target for the teeth. Morgan was swifter in retreat than the other man, but both jumped back from the snapping wolf. There was fury in Morgan's eyes as he picked up the stick that he used to push the water into the cage. He jabbed at Silverfeet, but the wolf ducked before the vicious point found his face.

"No need for that," the zoo man growled.

He bent down again and shone the light into the henhouse. He could see Silverfeet standing defiantly in the centre of the floor, facing the trapdoor. After a few minutes the man rose.

"O.K. I'll take him for seventy dollars. But how do you figure to get him out of there without losing an arm?"

"I already thought of that. I made me a catching pole. You know, one of them things with a noose at the end. I figure to open up the trapdoor like I did just now, wait for the varmint to come, and slip the noose over his head. It's wire, an' the pole's oak. Both will hold him. Then when he's played out, I can shove him back in the trapping cage."

"If you don't choke him to death," the other replied. "Tell you what, you get him caged and bring him to my place alive and in good shape, and you get the seventy bucks. O.K.?"

Morgan nodded and closed the trapdoor with the tip of his boot.

"Pay for the gas?" he asked.

"Yeah, I'll give you an extra five."

They shook hands, and the zoo man left. Morgan stood contemplating the door of the cage and there was pleasure in his eyes at the prospect of half-strangling the wolf.

8

Morgan rose early the next morning in anticipation of his battle with Silverfeet. After he had breakfasted, he donned a heavy bush coat and thick leather gloves, and went outside to fetch the crude catching pole he had made. He stood by the house examining the pole carefully. His heart was pumping fast and there was fear in him. But a thorough examination of the pole and its noose of braided wire reassured him. He had fashioned it after the kind used by humane society officials. It consisted of an eight-foot oak pole some two inches thick at the butt and tapering to an inch at the end, along the length of which he had fastened heavy metal eyelets. Through these ran the wire to a cleat secured to the end of the pole; the wire then doubled back through the cleat and was firmly secured to the wood. This formed a running noose which the man could tighten or slacken by adjusting his hold on the wire that ran down the pole. Once it was round the animal's neck, it could be held just tight enough to control the beast, to cut off its breath without killing it, if the operator was careful.

Morgan did not want to kill the wolf, but he did want revenge. He did not intend to be gentle. More than that, he was afraid. He was determined to choke the wolf within an inch of its life, to hold it in the stifling grasp of the noose until it became unconscious; then, and only then, would he open the henhouse door, pass the free end of the catching pole through the small trapdoor, and drag Silverfeet by the neck to the new cage he had placed outside the henhouse. Morgan tested the noose once again. It worked smoothly.

The man walked slowly towards the henhouse, the pole held in his right hand. In his mind there was fear, hate and greed; and as before, greed made him go forward when fear almost drove him back to get his rifle and use it against the wolf. He lingered over the short journey, excusing his slowness by telling himself that he did not want to alarm the wolf with sudden movement, yet all the time knowing that it was fear that was causing his steps to lag and all the time hating the wolf for creating this fear.

At last he stood three paces away from the henhouse door. He knew that Silverfeet had heard him. He knew as surely as if he could see him that the wolf was standing, waiting, lips curled back and ready to charge. Inwardly Morgan quaked. The moment had come and the remnants of his courage were leaving him. He forced himself to think of the seventy dollars, goading himself into action.

He had thought out his moves a thousand times already. He would open the trapdoor gently and stand back for a moment; then, deliberately, he would put a gloved hand just close enough to the opening to tempt the wolf to attack. He would then, he hoped, be able to slip the noose over the animal's head before he had time to draw it back.

Morgan bent to the catch on the trapdoor. Quietly he slipped it free, then eased the door open. He stood back. Nothing happened. Morgan moved forward again and slowly lowered his left hand, as though to reach inside the henhouse. In an instant Silverfeet's muzzle and those fearful teeth appeared in the opening. Morgan thrust at the wolf's head with the opened noose.

Instinct told Silverfeet that Morgan's approach was different that morning. He sensed trouble and was ready for it, so when he saw the reaching hand his attack was more vicious and more determined than before. Because of this he lingered just too long in the opening. When he saw and felt the wire he bit at it; and this was his undoing, for Morgan was able to slip the noose over his head and pull it tight.

Bedlam erupted inside the henhouse. A fierce growl ended in a strangled gasp as the wicked noose contracted, but the wolf had battle in him. He threshed and pulled wildly, contorting his body with such frenzy that twice he almost had his neck broken.

Morgan, white of face and fearful, could only try to hold on to the pole. Once the wolf's mad struggles almost pulled it out of his hands, but slowly, the man and his pole and his choking noose began to win, as Silverfeet's convulsed body lost power.

Inside the mind of the wolf there was a panic like no other he had ever felt. The thing about his neck was inexorable. He could not bite it, he could not intimidate it with his growls. He could only try to wrench free from its deadly hold. His breath was a grating torture; his throat, already bruised by the noose, felt on fire; his stomach convulsed and attempted to void its contents, but his throat was closed and only a thin trickle of bile erupted in spray through his nostrils. Still he fought, but his struggles were weak. Grayness filled his eyes, a kaleidoscope of lights coursed through his brain. He fell on his side and tried feebly to rise. At last he was still. His breath came slow and rasping. Then even this sound sank to a pathetic whisper.

Morgan was smiling broadly. Fear had left him. The wolf was at his mercy and he enjoyed his moment of triumph. He wanted to savour to the full this victory against his enemy. He kept the noose pulled tight.

Presently Morgan began to worry. Had he killed the wolf? He slackened the noose slightly and waited. A weak gasp followed. He slackened the noose still further and by bending low was able to see that Silverfeet's chest was moving slightly. The wolf was still alive.

Now was the time. Again tightening the noose, Morgan lifted the catch on the henhouse door and opened it, maintaining his grip on the pole, but allowing it to slide through the trap. When the door was open some six inches he peered inside. Silverfeet lay inert, stretched out on his side, but Morgan saw that he was not quite dead.

The man opened the door wide, shifting his grip on the pole from his left hand to his right. At last he had passed the butt of the pole through the trap and he was ready to drag the nearly dead wolf to the cage that he had placed near the henhouse the previous night. The sliding door was up, in position to slam down as soon as he released the noose from the animal's neck.

Again Morgan relaxed the noose just enough to allow a little air to enter the wolf's lungs. Silverfeet's breathing was mechanical, life stubbornly clinging to a body not yet quite dead.

He remained unmoving, but his body responded to the little oxygen that now reached it. The blackness that had filled his brain turned to grayness. The wolf became semi-conscious; but he was too weak to move.

Morgan began dragging Silverfeet. The noose tightened and again cut off the air, but when the wolf's body flopped onto the ground, the noose slackened slightly and a little more precious oxygen entered his struggling lungs.

Silverfeet was heavy. Morgan knew that he had to be careful not to break the wolf's neck. He eased the limp body slowly towards the cage, pausing often enough to allow the animal to breathe a little. Soon he had Silverfeet beside the entrance to the cage. This was the moment that Morgan had dreaded most. To get the wolf into the cage, he had to put him in with his hands. He had to let go of the pole and turn the wolf around so that his hindquarters would enter the trap first.

Morgan hesitated, his mind full of dread. His hesitation

allowed Silverfeet more air and somewhere in the wolf's dulled mind the instinct of life responded. Consciousness slowly filtered into Silverfeet's brain while Morgan wrestled with his fear. But Silverfeet stayed quiet.

Morgan bent, still holding the pole. He hesitated, then he dropped the pole, grasped Silverfeet's back legs and swivelled him around. Quickly he went to the wolf's shoulders and pushed him into the trap, until only his head protruded from the cage. Morgan again took the pole in his hand and he tried to push the wolf far enough inside to allow the drop-gate to close. Now! Swiftly he bent down to loosen the noose. It slipped off Silverfeet's neck and Morgan started to rise, reaching for the trip that would lower the gate.

At that instant the wolf's eyes opened. Morgan met with horror the baleful yellow gaze. He stood transfixed for perhaps five seconds.

Five fleeting, precious flecks of time turned the balance in favour of the moribund wolf. Without the murderous noose around his neck Silverfeet was able to draw great gulps of air into his lungs and the stubborn spark of life took advantage of the air and the moments of time.

Drunkenly Silverfeet rolled over from his side to his chest, finding purchase for his back legs against the wire bottom of the cage. The trap could not close against him. His head and part of his shoulders were outside the door.

Morgan's face became ashen. He knew with a dreadful certainty that the wolf was going to get away; he knew with terror that Silverfeet intended to even the score between them. Fear bit deep into Morgan's bowels. He might have saved himself by taking immediate, decisive action. But he could not. The yellow eyes of hate stopped him, the curled lips and ready fangs made his flesh crawl. In that instant, in his imagination, Morgan felt the fangs crunch into his body.

He stood as though frozen, his arms outstretched, his hands stilled in the act of reaching for the catches that held the drop-gate. Time stood still for Morgan, whose fear had robbed him of reason. But for the wolf, time was an ally. Silverfeet took advantage of it. He let his body rest, using only his lungs, drinking air as a thirsty man sucks up water. The indomitable vigour of the timber wolf struggled against great odds, and it won.

The moment of inaction passed. Silverfeet heaved his body upright and began moving forward, his bared teeth already reaching for the man. Morgan drew breath noisily and began to back away.

It happened then. Silverfeet, using every scrap of strength in his tortured body, launched himself at Morgan.

The wolf's front paws hit Morgan square in the chest. Man and wolf crashed to the ground. Morgan screamed. Silverfeet's growl was but a fraction lower than the man's hysteria. The next three minutes were a confused blur of movement and sound. The man and the wolf were as one swiftly-threshing body.

The contest was short. Snapping, slashing fangs were buried again and again in the man's body. Two fingers were torn from Morgan's right hand as it sought to ward off the terrible jaws. His left forearm was ripped open. The vengeful teeth closed on his throat.

Silverfeet clamped his jaws. Morgan's scream became a gurgle, a rattle, a liquid gasp. His body convulsed; the back arched, the legs jerked, and the heels beat upon the earth.

At last, mercifully, Morgan lay still. And the wolf slumped over the body of his enemy.

Half an hour later, Silverfeet staggered upright and hung his head, his eyes fixed on the dead man. The wolf was weak. He trembled, and he laboured for breath that did not want to pass by the torture in his throat. In his mouth the blood of his foe tasted bitter, unlike the warm fluids of the game he had once hunted.

After Morgan's struggles had ceased, Silverfeet had been too weak to move away and his instincts had told him to lie still, to build up his strength for the dash into freedom. Now, he was ready to go.

He was hungry, but he could not bring himself to eat of the

hated being that he had slain. He was thirsty, but he could not linger in this place of awful memory. He began to move, slowly, clumsily, a thin, dishevelled caricature of his former self. But he was free. The henhouse no longer confined him; the air outside was sweet, albeit still tainted by the scent of man. It was clean air, not fouled by ancient chicken droppings, not thick with the stench of his own stale wastes.

He walked northwards, mysterious urgings guiding him towards the boreal forests that were his heritage, and as he stumbled along, the memory of his sufferings and of the chilling fight goaded him. He wanted to run, to unleash his body into the lithe, mile-eating lope that had once been his; but he could not. He was a cripple, a half-dead thing sustained only by will; a creature persecuted by thoughts of horror, fettered by his sufferings, so that the mind that had been able to sustain him during the height of his physical hurts threatened to slip away permanently into witless limbo. But his legs kept moving. His lungs, seeming to have a will of their own, continued working, sucking in and puffing out, putting oxygen back into his blood.

For an hour he walked through scrubland that held scant cover. Twice he saw farm buildings in the distance and he skulked by them with fear pumping his heart. Once a dog barked at him but dared not leave the safety of his porch to chase a wolf.

At last, exhausted, he crawled under the thorny shelter of a dwarf juniper bush, a place that he would normally have avoided because of the small, sharp needles that forced their way under his coat and scratched at his skin. It was the only cover that he could find and he could not go on. He closed his eyes and sleep came to him. Overhead the weak sunshine pierced the last shreds of morning mist, highlighting the tracks that Silverfeet had left on the muddy ground.

It was afternoon and the zoo man had become impatient with Morgan, who had promised to deliver the wolf by noon of that day. The trapper's failure had brought the zoo man to Morgan's isolated house. He sounded his car horn as he got out from behind the steering wheel, and began walking towards the ramshackle dwelling. Then he saw Morgan's outstretched body. He knew at once what had happened. He did not want to approach the body, but he forced himself to go near and he made himself look at the maimed throat, and he even reached down and placed a hand over the still heart. He was white of face when he rose upright and turned away to run for his car. Without a backward glance at what had been Morgan he turned the machine around and raced out of the yard. He drove fast all the way to town and there he found the police and reported his finding.

For five hours Silverfeet remained curled under the juniper, gripped by the sleep of exhaustion. It was late afternoon when he awoke suddenly. Already the light was failing and the clouds which had swept over the region for most of that day had slowed their course and hung gray and compact over the land. Rain would soon come. The wolf lay unmoving for some moments. Something had penetrated the haze of his sleep and had alerted the trigger-taut instincts that are the heritage of the hunting wolf.

He listened, his ears pricked upright and swivelling, and gradually a sound that would have defied human hearing caused him to scramble out from under the bush, turn towards the south and stand statue-stiff, head raised, scanning the far distance. In another moment he changed direction and forced his stiff body into a fast lope, pointing again to the north. The faint sound continued to pursue him. He knew it for what it was, the sound made by the thing that had carried him to the trapper's house.

The hum of an automobile engine immediately awakened memories of Morgan, of the trap, of the horror of the journey in the back of the truck, and of his seemingly endless days of captivity in the dark, sour henhouse. He could not, of course, reason over the sound, but experience had taught him that the growl of an engine was invariably accompanied by the presence of man.

Silverfeet did not know that the machine at his back contained three men armed with rifles who were even then seeking him; he did not know this, but still he ran, knowing that man's presence meant for him fear and danger. He had learned his lesson. He would never forget it. He would never bury his hatred for the creatures that walked tall and carried the nauseating scent.

Before his capture Silverfeet would have avoided man, but he would have done so with little more than a wild creature's casual alarm when human sound or sight penetrated its domain. Things were different now. Silverfeet's hate burned deep. Where once he would only have sought escape or, if cornered, attempted to bluff his way out with growls and the baring of teeth, now, if his freedom was threatened, he would spring for the throat and he would kill. Morgan had done this to him. This was the trapper's legacy.

And there was more to it than that. Unknown to the wolf, Morgan's death had turned him into a pariah. From now on, unless he was able to break away from the scattered civilization that surrounded him, the hand of every man would be against him; men with cars and guns, men on foot with dogs, men in aircraft would hunt the killer wolf. Relentlessly, unfairly, they would seek revenge. It mattered not that Morgan had been the aggressor, depriving the wolf of his precious freedom and treating him cruelly and hatefully. It was of no importance that the wolf had responded instinctively, in the only way he knew, to the fear and hatred implanted in him by the man. To his pursuers only one thing was clear: a wolf had killed a man and this could not be tolerated. Silverfeet had committed an unforgivable sin.

They hunted him now and because the country was flat and there was scant cover, the three in the four-wheel-drive vehicle were gaining on him, even though they had to stop often to check his tracks. And in the sky a government service helicopter was turning on the same course, guided by the men in the vehicle, who had signalled the pilot by radio. Only the fast-coming darkness offered hope to the exhausted wolf.

His lope had dwindled to little more than a walk. He was weak, his body hurt and his front feet were bleeding, for the badly-healed toes had opened anew.

Once he stopped and stared over his shoulder into the gloom and he saw the twin pinpoints of light that came from the pursuing machine. He forced himself to run faster, ignoring his wounds and the pain in his chest. He gulped air jerkily, painfully, for his swollen throat restricted his breathing. But he ignored these things and set his mind to the task of eluding his pursuers.

At first he did not separate the sound of the automobile engine from the roar of the helicopter. Then he directed his gaze to the sky and he saw it, like a strange bird, coming fast, its navigation lights adding terror to the thing.

He was lucky. The low cloud cover and the lateness of the day helped his body blend into the colour and contours of the earth. The two men in the helicopter did not see him as they passed over him, though they were flying a mere hundred feet from the ground. The cataclysmal roar of the rotors, the down-draft they created, and the sudden swooshing sound immediately over him caused Silverfeet to swing off his northerly course, ducking wildly towards the west. And luck again helped him.

He had almost reached the shelter of a willow break that bordered a small stream when the pilot sighted him and turned the aircraft. In another instant the helicopter swept over him again, but this time the passenger was leaning out of the plastic bubble, a loaded shotgun in his hand. Silverfeet dodged just as the gunner squeezed the triggers, firing both barrels almost simultaneously. Had the wolf swerved a second later the end would have come then. As it was, only one pea-sized pellet hit Silverfeet, raking his ribs and opening a shallow furrow in his skin.

The burning pain of the wound, the bark of the gun and the din of the helicopter's engines drove the wolf to extremes of which he would otherwise not have been capable. Instinct made him run a zig-zag course and the remnants of sanity in his mind directed him to make for the willows no more than fifty yards away.

As the helicopter turned to come in for the kill, Silverfeet thrust his body into the tangle of riverbank growth. The shadows were deeper in there, and the wolf disappeared from sight. The helicopter pilot radioed his information and said he was turning back. It was too dark for the aircraft.

Silverfeet crouched trembling in the centre of the willow thicket. He licked at his wound and noted the retreat of the aircraft. But almost at the same moment he heard the approaching jeep. He moved deeper into his shelter, and found a tangle of brush that offered better concealment. Under this he squeezed his body. He was spent. If man was to find him, it would be in this place. The wolf crouched low and waited, all his senses keyed to the nearing danger.

Light flashed into the thicket as the vehicle slowed, then stopped. Voices reached Silverfeet and he bared his fangs.

"We should've brought the dogs," said one man.

"Yeah. Personally, I don't fancy going in there to look for him. Can't see a thing in the tangle and that animal's a killer," another man replied.

The third man was the one who had found Morgan's body, the zoo man. He felt the coldness of fear in his vitals.

"There's no way that you'll get me in that place, not with that beast on the loose. If he's holed up in there he could grab any one of us fast and the others couldn't shoot. No, I'm for letting it go tonight. We'll come out in the morning with the dogs and see if we can pick up his trail again," he said.

In his hiding place Silverfeet remained unmoving, listening to the voices that fanned his hate. Had the men been able to see the blaze in his eyes they would have known that their fears were justified. For a time they stood by their truck discussing the matter. At last they climbed into their vehicle and left.

When the sound of the engine had faded to a purr, Silverfeet left his hiding place and again pointed himself to the north. He was a sorry spectacle as he limped towards freedom. The wound in his side was not severe, but its stinging hurt added to his distress. It gaped bloody and raw, matting the hair on his side. It made breathing even more painful, for each time his chest and flanks heaved as he inhaled, the lips of the wound were stretched.

Of all his wounds, the recently-healed cuts on his front feet were the most dangerous to his safety. The scabs on his toes had broken open; the cut inflicted by the glass of the henhouse window was bleeding again. These things slowed his progress and left bloodstains on the ground, inviting pursuit when the men returned with tracking dogs.

A man in these circumstances, using his superior powers of reason, would have asked himself repeatedly why he had been subjected to so many brutal indignities. He would have wondered at the sadistic nature of the being who had set out deliberately to capture a creature of harmless intent who was merely trying to return to his own realm; who, indeed, would not have ventured out of his habitat had he and his kind not been driven away by fire.

Silverfeet's mind was not encumbered with these speculations. He had but one thought: freedom. This drove him onwards despite his crippling hurts; it dulled the hate that he felt for man; it even helped to ease his pain and his hunger.

He had stopped to drink from the cold waters of the stream, slaking his thirst fully for the first time since his capture. This had revived him, and allowed him to go on. Without that opportune water, Silverfeet would have died in that place.

An hour after he left the shelter of the willows, full darkness came, aiding the fugitive in his slow, stealthy passage between two large farms. Had he been stronger, he would have circled them, but tonight he could not afford the time and energy that such a move would demand. He was not, of course, consciously aware that the men would renew their chase with daylight, but his instincts told him that danger lay in wait throughout the entire area of man's domain.

He could not stop, though his body was just one degree short of total exhaustion. Nor could he allow himself the wide detours he would normally have used in order to avoid the haunts of man. So he skulked silently from scrubby bush to irregular boulder, seeming to slide along the ground, to disappear totally in the hollows of the earth.

He was almost past the first house when the barking of a dog disturbed the quiet. Silverfeet had never seen a dog, but he knew that the animal raising this alarm was an enemy. He remembered that he had been barked at before. He did not want to meet this creature.

He forced himself to go faster. He was clear of the house and about to enter an area of scattered evergreens when he realized that the barking was nearer. The dog was giving chase — foolishly, for he was alone. The dog had never met a wolf either, but this intruder must be chased away.

Silverfeet knew he could not outdistance the dog so he backed into the shelter of a balsam tree whose lower branches swept almost to the ground. Here the wolf waited, his back protected, his fangs ready to meet whatever was coming towards him.

At the last moment the conflict was avoided. The dog was but ten paces from the wolf when a whistle pierced the air and a man's voice called him. But the whistle and the call alone would not have stopped the dog. It was a hidden instinct, an ancient warning that made him stop, probe the scent of the stranger, and quickly turn for home. In another instant he was racing back towards the house, frightened, his tail tucked between his legs, glad to obey his master's summons. Silverfeet came out of hiding, paused to stare in the direction of the farmhouse and continued slowly on his way.

The wolf's sufferings had become intense. He felt himself driven onwards although his every instinct told him to stop, to sleep, to recuperate and to find prey. He needed food desperately and he needed rest as badly. It was fortunate that nature had designed the wolf so well, had given the species the endurance of iron and the determination to resist defeat even when death appeared imminent. But there was a limit to all things and this thin, hurt, desperate wolf was rapidly reaching his. Gamely he continued walking, always heading north, forever scanning the route ahead, seeking cover, smelling for game, which he still hoped to be able to bring down, though it was doubtful that he had enough strength left to make a large kill. He would not give in. Could he this night find shelter and hiding against the hunt that would begin again in the morning? He did not dwell on this question; he simply forged on, limping, panting, aching, bleeding. He was indomitable, every fibre of him denying defeat, every hidden source of strength being summoned to his aid.

He struggled on for several more hours, passing three more farms without raising an alarm, and gradually he neared a treed region that offered better cover than the open fields and marshy bushlands over which he had passed. Towards dawn he reached the trees, and luck was with him. He had stumbled upon a low-lying wooded section of land that, useless for agriculture, had been abandoned for many years. Age and storms had furnished many places of shelter where trees had crashed, one across the other, to form an almost impassable lattice of jungle-like decay. Into this labyrinth Silverfeet eased his failing body, pushing it towards the centre of the largest tangle as he searched for a secure hideout. His tracks became indistinct in the marshy, soaking land and his scent was diluted by the strong odours of rotting vegetation and marsh gases.

Before him was a large, dead elm that had been torn loose from its anchorage by a storm. It had toppled earthward, tearing its bell-like root system out of the ground, the interwoven roots still clinging to clods of earth and small rocks and tendrils of aquatic plants. Under the overhang of the roots nature had eroded a small, cave-like place. It was wet and cramped, but it was a perfect refuge. Stopping only long enough to quench his thirst from a pool of brown, stagnant water, Silverfeet crawled under the roots. He curled himself into a tight ball of misery and closed his eyes. Within seconds he was asleep.

He was awakened by the baying of hounds during late afternoon of the next day. At first his bemused senses did not know what to make of the bell-like tones of the hunting dogs. He stayed in his shelter, his senses slowly returning. He listened. The hounds were close, perhaps half a mile to the south, but Silverfeet's keen ears could not detect the presence of man.

He rose and went to quench his thirst again. Although his body was stiff and sore, the long sleep had restored some of his lost energy. After drinking, he stood and faced the clamour of the dogs, deciding on the course that he should follow. He felt stronger, still he knew that he could not outrun the pack that was searching for him. So he crawled back under the root, wedging himself tightly into the small space so that only his head and shoulders were vulnerable to attack. And, resting his head on his paws, he waited for whatever was to come.

More than a mile away, to the south, the three men of yesterday had stopped their vehicle and were preparing to follow their dogs on foot. Each carried a gun, all were determined to kill the wolf that, in their minds, was a vicious, blood-mad menace. To the west and to the east, similar groups of men with dogs were scouring the country for sign of the wolf. The entire neighbourhood had been alerted and all men living in the area were eager to join in the hunt. Some felt that the wolf must be destroyed because it had killed one of their kind, and this, to them, was justice. Others joined for the fun of the thing. All of them wanted the life of the wolf.

Already rumours had spread accusing the wolf of every conceivable crime. The farmer whose dog had chased Silverfeet last night swore that the wolf had entered his yard and tried to kill his dog. Another farmer assured his listeners that he had narrowly escaped attack the night before as he was going to his barn; the only thing that saved him, this man claimed, was that he had been able to get into the barn and slam the door in the wolf's face. The hunters did not stop to examine the truth of these stories, which served only to fan their hatred of the wolf.

It was ever thus. The unusual has power to excite the imagination of some people who, perhaps seeking an importance that they do not normally have, conjure up events which have never taken place but which, after a time, take on the proportions of truth within the minds of their originators.

These things were now of no consequence. What mattered was that a community of people had been aroused by what seemed to them to be the wanton killing of one of their kind. Even though not many of them had held any special regard for Morgan, the lust to kill, which lurks just under the surface of the human mind, had been released. The hunters wanted blood, and they intended to get it.

The group that was closest to Silverfeet's hiding place paused on the edge of the wooded marsh, listening to the bugle calls of their dogs. They knew by the hounds' voices that the scent was fresh, but they also knew that the dogs had not yet found the wolf. Faced by the almost impenetrable barrier of downed timber and spongy moss, they hesitated, remaining on high ground.

The zoo man turned to his two companions.

"That's pretty tough country in there," he said, speaking more to himself than to the others.

"Yeah," one of them replied. "Perhaps the dogs will flush him out. I hope so. Don't fancy wading in through that lot."

The third man lifted his rifle, pumped a shell into its chamber and fired a shot high over the trees.

"Mebbe if we take pot shots in there he'll break cover," he said, by way of explaining his action.

The other two nodded and, one at a time, they fired their rifles into the woods.

Silverfeet stayed where he was. The dogs had lost his scent and he, experienced hunter that he was, knew this by the way they had scattered. Two had gone beyond his hiding place; the third, a grizzled veteran of many hunts, was still casting about, circling, snuffling at the ground with determination. He was the most dangerous of the three and Silverfeet knew this.

Suddenly the hound's voice became deeper and more urgent in its pitch. He had struck the trail; and he ran on it, the fever of the hunt making him reckless. Ten minutes later he found Silverfeet. He stopped just outside the root overhang and called in earnest. He was answered immediately by the other two dogs who were by then almost half a mile away.

The dog and the wolf stared at one another, the hound noisy in his bugling, the wolf silent, deadly, his fangs ready. Suddenly Silverfeet hurled himself at the dog.

His rush was so sudden and swift that the hound was unable to either dodge it or meet it. In an instant Silverfeet's fangs had fastened over the dog's jugular vein. Moments later, without even a yelp, the hound lay dead, his throat torn. In this place, Silverfeet knew, the odds were with him. This was his kind of country; here the wolf was king, not man, not even his dogs.

Silverfeet left the dead hound and went out to meet the second dog, who was approaching from the northwest. He ignored the third dog who was more distant and coming in from the east. The wolf's fighting instincts were so aroused that he no longer felt his wounds or the effect of his long fast. He had slept well and soundly and sleep had lent him the strength that he needed.

The hound advertised his presence with his loud voice. The wolf walked wraithlike to meet him, always seeking cover, moving slowly and purposefully. Soon only some forty yards separated the two, but they could not see each other through the denseness of the woods. The advantage, the knowledge and the experience were with the wolf. He sidestepped and crouched behind a tangle of fallen trees. There he waited. And when the dog came rushing by, Silverfeet leaped upon him and closed his fangs in the back of his neck. The hound yelped in fear and pain. For a few moments after that both animals struggled, growling. The fight ended quickly. Silverfeet released his hold just as the hound overbalanced. The dog fell, rolled and started to rise, but the wolf came in quickly for the kill. His mouth found the soft underpart of the neck and the dog died.

The men on the edge of the woods knew what had happened when they heard the dog cry out. So did the third hound. He had reached the body of the pack leader and he stopped beside it, raising his voice loudly, calling to the men. The hunters cursed and began to scramble frantically through the tangled growth. But by then Silverfeet was running northward, putting distance between himself and his pursuers.

The hunt ended then. The men knew that with only one dog they could not hope to bring the wolf to bay. They knew also that they were facing a formidable creature, an animal crazed by suffering, fear and hate.

On that afternoon a legend was born, which was to live for many years in that country, growing bigger with the passing of time. It was to tell of the mad wolf that one day had come out of the forest to kill a defenceless trapper, eat his body, and then turn upon the dogs of the community. It was to tell of the enormous creature that had terrorized the farmers for weeks at a time. Yes, the legend was to grow and the untruths were to become embellished and the fear and hatred that man has felt for the wolf since time began was to live upon these festering falsehoods until it found its way into the pages of the newspapers and the whole land read them and believed them, and some men, banding into groups, called for the extermination of every wolf in the land. But this was to come later, long after Silverfeet had found his way back to his wilderness.

9

The young muskrat walked humped up and ungainly, looking for a place in which to den. He was one of the many creatures who, every year, are turned out of their birthplaces and forced to seek living quarters for themselves in other parts of the wild. This one had wandered far in his quest. He had inspected likely bank dens along the northern length of the creek in which he was born, only to be repulsed ferociously by their occupants. He had stopped often in marsh and beaver pond to check some of the small muskrat lodges, but each time he had found these places occupied and had been forced to retreat.

When Silverfeet saw him he was crossing an open meadow, heading for another marsh. He was so anxious to find sanctuary before the snow fell, that he had become careless.

The wolf quickly cut him off and held him at bay. But the muskrat had courage. He stood on his back legs, squealed and gnashed his teeth, jumping for Silverfeet every time he went in for the kill. Had the wolf been healthy, the battle would have been over in seconds. As it was, Silverfeet's movements were slow and clumsy. Twice the rat's chisel teeth fastened on the wolf's upper lip; twice Silverfeet shook his head, sending the rat flying to crash several feet away. But Silverfeet persisted. He had to eat or die. He saw to it that the agile rat could not escape, and waited until it became tired from its furious exertions. Then his jaws found it, and it died.

Silverfeet ate his prize slowly. Normally he would have pulled off most of the rat's fur with his teeth, but tonight he crunched through fur, skin, bones, and meat, and swallowed all of it. When he had finished he licked himself clean, crossed the meadow, and disappeared amongst the evergreens that crowned the top of a ridge. He was exhausted, and his only thought, now that he had eaten, was to find a secure place in which to sleep.

After a time he bedded under a newly-fallen spruce, bellying his way under the thick cluster of green branches to a place that afforded perfect concealment. He slept through that night and all the next day and when he awoke at sundown he looked different.

He was still lean and his wounds were raw and sore, but the meagre meal of muskrat and the long sleep had worked wonders. No longer did he carry his tail tucked despondently between his legs; he did not flinch in pain when he sucked air into his lungs. Instead he carried his brush high and he held his head up and his ears were constantly on the move, alert for prey.

He had not forgotten the men and the dogs; he never forgot them. But he felt safe now. This was his country. Here and there were tall trees and deep, dark tangles that offered concealment. No roaring monster could reach him from the sky and the other machines of man could not enter into the land of trees. Dogs could follow him, but he felt no fear of them. He could deal with them as he had done yesterday; he could ambush them, one at a time, and destroy them. But he needed more food.

It was late afternoon when Silverfeet killed again. This time a snowshoe hare was his victim, but only by luck. The hare had been resting in its form under a downed tree, and the wind had favoured the wolf. The hare would have escaped, for Silverfeet was still too weak to match the creature's formidable speed. But so startled was the hare when it noticed the wolf but a few paces away that it leaped too hurriedly, hurtling headlong into a tree. Before it could recover Silverfeet was upon it. Again he ate slowly and felt a surge of new strength.

At sundown he surprised a fox that had killed another hare and he took the prize away from him. This time, when he had finished eating, he felt almost satisfied. He decided to sleep.

A week passed. The wolf was in better condition now that his pace was not being forced by pursuit, but he still went hungry more often than he fed. He was too slow for most game.

During this time he continued to head north, putting a few more miles between himself and civilization every day. The going was slow because he was forced to hunt almost constantly, patiently stalking mice or squirrels. Occasionally he managed to surprise a hare, and once he took a grouse that had been injured by shotgun pellets and could not fly. Day after day he edged his way towards the big country of spruce and pine and tamarack, lonely for the sight and sound of his kind.

Twice he made detours to avoid lonely farms. During the second detour he saw a man moving about the farmyard and the great hate that he still carried with him welled up and brought a snarl to his lips. He kept travelling, forever on the alert for prey, but seldom getting anything more substantial than a hare, almost daily having to do with mice, each of which offered hardly a mouthful.

When he awoke from a long sleep on the morning of the eighth day he found himself in a new world. Snow had fallen steadily all night and it lay soft and white and five inches deep in the open places of the forest. It was the cold of the snow that woke Silverfeet who, for the first time in his short life, felt the chill of winter against a coat that was still thin, and bare where he had rubbed it against the mesh of his cage. The snow made his feet hurt and the unhealed wound in his side throbbed from it. In exchange, it offered him only one blessing, he could eat it and quench his thirst without having to go in search of water.

He stood and shook the snow from his body and he shivered. He felt alone and melancholy. He howled; but his wail elicited no reply. Five times he howled before he stretched and started trotting towards the north.

All morning he kept moving, stopping rarely to hunt for food, and finding none. By early afternoon he topped a rise and saw below him the whitened surface of a large beaver pond. Presently his eyes caught movement on the far bank and he noted that the water was open at that place. Momentarily he lost sight of the dark body that had attracted his attention, then he saw it again. It was a beaver, still toiling to drag supplies of poplar to its winter storage place in the mud of the lake bottom.

Here was meat in plenty if he could get to it. Cautiously he backed off the high land and slunk into the forest, selecting the northern side of the pond because it was downwind of where he had seen the beaver. He travelled as quickly as he could, exerting the utmost caution. At last he was close enough to the beaver's slipway to smell the musk of his prey.

He walked, his body held in a half crouch, redoubling his caution. Soon he heard the beaver as it gnawed at a branch of a downed poplar, and he knew that his presence had so far gone undetected. Guided by the sound he crept on, inching his way, the slobber of anticipation filling his mouth. He was almost sure of the kill. He stood between the beaver and the lake and, slow as he was, he knew that he could outrun this creature on land. In the water the beaver could escape effortlessly, but here it was hindered by its short legs and by its rolling, ungainly pace.

Silverfeet saw the beaver. It was standing on its hind legs, chopping through a six-inch limb. Its back was towards the wolf. Silverfeet waited no longer. He growled, loudly, to put fear into the rodent's mind, and charged straight for the prey. The beaver dropped on all fours and whirled, attempting to run for the water. Silverfeet let him go by for a few clumsy paces. Being fearful of the beaver's great chopping teeth, he preferred to attack this fat creature from the back. In two bounds he straddled the beaver and seized it by the back of the neck. He bit deep and clenched his jaws, knowing that the beaver would fight and knowing, too, that he was weak and the beaver was strong.

Fighting for his life, the beaver threshed his forty-pound body. This was his only defence against the wolf's attack. Silverfeet almost lost his hold, but slowly his killing grip began to tell and the beaver's struggles grew less. Five minutes later the beaver was dead and Silverfeet lay beside it, exhausted but content. Presently he gorged, and when he stopped he was full for the first time in almost three weeks. He had eaten more than half the kill; the warm meat rounded his shrunken belly and it felt good.

After cleaning his muzzle and chest, he licked at his front paws. They were becoming hardened by travel. On each toe a vestige of new nail showed and most of the scabs had given way to scar tissue. The cut on his pad was still troublesome, but it was healing also. So was his side, which was well scabbed and had lost its soreness. This day Silverfeet felt contentment. He lay beside the remains of his kill and he yawned. His cavernous jaws opened wide, and closed with a snap. A slight whine of pleasure escaped from his throat. And this, too, was a new sensation; the hurt of the noose was almost gone. He decided to sleep next to the kill.

A crescent of moon hung in the blue-black sky when Silverfeet opened his eyes and moved slightly, disturbing a marauding mouse who had been feasting on the beaver's remains. The wolf made no attempt to chase the tiny scavenger, who squeaked fear and scurried away into the whitened underbrush. Nearby a great horned owl sat in a tree and called in its hoarse voice. Silverfeet looked up, trying to spot the night raider but failing to find him. The wolf felt good. He stood, stretched till his very bones snapped, yawned, shook his coat to loosen the hair. Then he settled down to finish the remains of his kill.

It was time to move, for the northland called and the wolf was anxious to find his home range. Night was his time and this night offered a new freedom to Silverfeet. He had eaten well and his wounds were almost healed. If he could run well, he might reach true wilderness by morning. He set out at a good lope, moving with greater ease than he had done since his escape. Around him the night glowed and the sounds of dark were trusted companions to the running wolf. Three times he stopped to rest and once he broke ice at a small beaver pond and drank greedily. By dawn he had reached muskeg country. This was wilderness. Here, he knew, he would find other wolves. The journey had been long, but he had survived its dangers. He was free, fully free, at last.

Deep winter had come, bringing its cold and its snows and its biting winds. It was mid-December. The wilderness was held fast in the brittle grip of freeze-up. But life persisted.

Under the deep snow the mice scurried through their glacial tunnels as they journeyed from feeding haunts to nest chambers, reasonably secure from the hunters of night. By day, red squirrels ransacked the forest, ever alert for overlooked pine cones, or for a cache that one of their own kind had hidden carelessly.

In the sheltered places of the forest, where the evergreens mantled the floor with their spreading branches, the snow was less deep and was criss-crossed with a variety of tracks. Weasel, marten, fisher; fox, wolverine, deer; squirrel, grouse, jay; all had left their marks.

Here and there remnants of death lingered. A bundle of feathers and a stain of blood told of a grouse that had died under the talons of an owl or between the teeth of fox or weasel. Patches of scattered fur and deep imprints of lynx or bobcat told their own story of hunger and life and death.

The trees stood in serried clusters, their branches weighted down with snow. In these trees were the birds of the northland. The gray jays, at times raucous, at times sweet-voiced mimics, could spy food no matter how cunningly concealed. The little, fluffed-up chickadees with their bright faces and black caps called their names as they bustled about in the evergreens searching for insect eggs and other tidbits. The nuthatches, with hoarse, nasal voices and thin, black beaks, walked upside down on trunk or branch as easily as they walked upright.

These were the creatures of winter. Creation had fashioned them well and had given their bodies the strength to withstand the time of the great cold. Inevitably some died before spring came to bring new growth and new life, but, aloof from man in this vastness of forest and river and lake there always remained enough of each species to start anew each year, to mate and to give birth, to ensure that the species did not perish.

This was the kingdom of Silverfeet, but it was a lonely one, a realm unshared by his own kind. He cried his nostalgia night after night. With head upraised he launched his wild, sad cry, always hoping to receive an answer.

The wolf had gained strength, had put on weight and had grown in girth. His old hurts were fully healed. His coat was prime, the long, shining guard hairs and the fine, thick, silken underfur insulating his body against all that a northland winter could conjure. With food in his belly and the boundless vitality of nature to protect him, the young wolf was secure in his wilderness.

It is true that there were times when the hunting was bad, when it seemed that luck had deserted him, but hungry nights and days are normal to a hunting wolf. He could endure them now that he had fully recovered from the depredations of Morgan and his neighbours. And then he would strike and he would gorge and his body would store energy, building itself up for the next time of failure. This was his natural life, this was the way of the wild, and he understood it.

His loneliness was something else. This he could not understand and he found it hard to endure. He had been fashioned to run with a pack; deep social instincts drove him towards the communal unit, where each shared in feast and in famine, in hardship and in ease; where the silent companionship made endurable the coldest night, the most bowel-gnawing hunger.

He still remembered his own pack: his mother, his father and his small black sister. And at these times he thought of the one who had parted him from them, and the hate grew in him like some flesh-eating ulcer. He vented it on the prey that he hunted, tearing, growling and snapping at his victims long after he had killed them, as though seeking to cleanse himself of an emotion that only man can instill.

Normally Silverfeet, like all wild creatures, would not have known the meaning of hate. He would have killed fiercely but dispassionately when hunger drove him onto the hunting trail; he would have fought without rancour over some morsel of food that another member of the pack wanted; he would have braved the rivalry of his own kind during the mating season. But whatever violence came his way would have been suffered or inflicted philosophically, because it was necessary, not because there was hatred in his heart, or vengeance in his mind.

The hate that had been aroused in him by Morgan would linger until the wilderness, in its compassion, restored him fully to himself.

As a sphere of orange sun dispelled the shadows of pre-dawn, Silverfeet crept from his den under a downed spruce only two hours after he had curled up for sleep. He had hunted well last night, cornering an ailing deer in a deep snowdrift and effecting a quick kill. As was his custom he had gorged until his belly was distended, then he had sought shelter and settled for what usually would have been a long sleep. But restlessness woke him and he stood and stretched his powerful frame, going through the waking ritual quite unconscious of his actions, his mind occupied with a deep nostalgia.

When he had finished he sat and howled, waited a moment and howled again. When no answer came he trotted away from the shelter of his bed, pausing just long enough to pick fastidiously at the remains of the deer, and then turned towards the north. He kept loping all through that day, unable to fathom the thing that drove him, only forced to obey its commands. And so he ran until night and fatigue stopped him. Then, finding a shelter, he curled his body, nose to tail, closed his eyes and slept.

All through that night he remained a tight ball of breathing fur, but when the sun tipped the trees he set out, northwards again, his tail hanging low, his head and nose pointing downwards to the snow. In this way he ran for an hour.

Suddenly he stopped. He had reached a place of numerous tracks and his nose told him that these had been made by a pack of wolves. Into his eyes came a gleam of joy; his tail wagged for the first time in many weeks. He sniffed at the tracks for a moment, ran on a few paces, following them, and stopped again at a place in the snow which was yellow with urine. Ecstatically, he put his nose upon the stain and inhaled the rankness of wolf. In an instant he dropped onto the snow and began to roll over the place, his eyes half lidded in joy, his lips peeled back in a thin smile of pleasure. At last, after one great kick at air with all four paws, he bounded to his feet and, nose to the trail, ran swiftly after the pack.

Half an hour later he found the wolves resting within the shelter of a tight ring of spruces. He stopped before he saw them, and let their odours penetrate his mind through his nostrils. And within the trees the resting pack scented Silverfeet's presence.

At first the six wolves merely lifted their heads and pricked up their ears, then the pack leader, a brindled dog, rose and stood facing the place where he knew Silverfeet waited. The five other wolves rose also. They watched their leader and, one by one, lifted their hackles as he had done and stood silent and stiff, waiting for the stranger to show himself. This was a ritual as old as time itself; it said clearly that this pack judged cautiously, with mixed feelings, the stranger that had come.

When Silverfeet stepped softly into view, their attitude did not change. The pack was tense, not yet aggressive, but showing that it was ready to attack this stranger if the leader's whim so decided. This is the way of the wolves. A stranger of their own kind may or may not be accepted, depending on the mood of the pack and of the stranger. Perhaps it is a matter of chemistry, or personality; whatever the reason, a strange wolf approaching a new pack is never sure of his reception. And although Silverfeet had never before encountered such a situation, his instincts told him that he must use caution; that, eager though he was to become a part of this pack, he must obey the ancient ritual and abide by the pack law.

He strode slowly towards the six wolves. His movements were humble; the way in which he carried his body showed submission to the will of the pack. But his tail wagged eagerly, offering friendship, and his black-lined lips peeled back in a lupine smile. After a few yards he stopped, wagged his tail more vigorously, and whined, the noise both a greeting and an appeal.

Some members of the pack began to relax; one twitched his tail in a half wag. It seemed as though to them Silverfeet was acceptable. But the big leader retained his aggressive posture, his hackles, if anything, becoming stiffer, his slit-eyed gaze more intent. He took a step towards Silverfeet, stopped, and growled. Immediately the rest of the pack stiffened again and viewed the stranger with more caution. Silverfeet advanced another three steps, still wagging his tail, whining now and then, showing himself to be friendly, offering himself to the pack.

Perhaps a faint scent of man still adhered to Silverfeet, or perhaps his size and obvious power posed a threat in the mind of the big brindled dog. Whatever the reason, the leader was not disposed to allow the stranger to join the pack. He growled again, and this seemed to signal the pack into action. The wolves moved forward and surrounded Silverfeet, who wagged the more, smiled, and bowed a greeting. This, too, was customary. Even when a pack was prepared to accept a newcomer, it first tested him, roughing him up, snapping a little and perhaps knocking him to the ground, before allowing him to take his place within its ranks. And again, Silverfeet knew this instinctively.

Suddenly, the leader charged at Silverfeet, hitting him with his right shoulder and knocking him down. Immediately the big dog snapped at one of Silverfeet's flailing legs. This started the other pack members, who at first offered only token aggression, their bites just hard enough to hurt, but not wicked enough to draw blood. Not so the pack leader. He bit at Silverfeet's exposed rump, sinking his teeth and drawing blood. The sight and smell of the wound put frenzy into the rest of the pack and Silverfeet, startled by the pain of the bite, found himself rolling and dodging under their feet as he tried to avoid the snapping, flashing teeth that sought him from all directions.

Silverfeet felt the change of mood. He knew that because of the pack leader he was not going to be accepted. He knew also that unless he escaped from the circle of snapping jaws he would be killed. He heaved himself upright, ignored the eager attacks of the pack members and faced the leader, his hate coming alive.

He attacked swiftly, instantly, knowing that to hesitate would mean death. He charged the brindled dog, snapped at his head as he thrust with his shoulder. The pack leader was flung back; he stumbled and fell, and Silverfeet's teeth ripped his left ear.

The pack was startled. They had expected the stranger to break for freedom, for this was normal. They had not expected him to attack as he fled. The sight of their leader's struggles to regain his footing, the blood on his ear, and the ferocity of the stranger's mien, immobilized them for a moment. In that time Silverfeet escaped, racing swiftly into the spruces. The wolves did not follow. They had rejected the newcomer; that was all that pack law required.

The hate that had kindled so quickly within him at the pack's refusal to accept him soon burned out of Silverfeet as he ran through the forest, and loneliness returned. An hour after his encounter with the wolves he stopped, sat down, and cried his anguish. He licked at his injuries, which were not severe. The worst was where the pack leader had sunk his teeth into his rump; this was stiff and sore, but it would not hinder him. After a time he moved on. He was hungry, so he moved with stealth, scenting constantly, stopping often to listen. By late afternoon he had run down and killed four snowshoe hares and his hunger was appeased. He settled for the night.

Three days later, Silverfeet was still travelling north through a land heavy with timber and rich in game, a boreal forest of stately beauty.

The young wolf had eaten well since his brush with the pack. The white hares were more plentiful than they had been the winter before, and easy to catch. But his longing for companionship seldom left him. He howled often and, while maintaining a northerly direction, he systematically quartered the forest, forever searching for another wolf pack. Occasionally he found old tracks and followed them for a time, eager and excited, only to stop and howl despondently when the tracks ended, covered by snow that had fallen days earlier.

One night he uncurled himself from his bedding place and looked up at the fullness of a sparkling moon. He was about to start out on a hunt, but something stopped him. He sat and contemplated the shining disc that highlighted the forest, and he howled, a long, deep mournful baying that rang through the trees and over the lakes and lost itself in space. As he ended his song, he hung his head, drew breath and began to point moonwards again, to vent his feelings a second time. Just at this point a chorus of answering howls came to him out of the night.

Silverfeet became transformed. For an instant his ears pricked forward and his lips peeled back in a smile, then he lifted his broad head and sang in full voice, a new note replacing the nostalgia that had been in his howl for so long. For a time he and the pack called to each other, then Silverfeet moved.

The pack was near; he knew this. He ran towards the sound of their calls and soon he was on the edge of their rendezvous. The howls had stopped; the pack had scented him, and now they waited quietly for the stranger to show himself. Silverfeet hesitated long enough to assure the wolves that he came in friendship, not wishing to startle them by a sudden appearance.

Presently he moved towards the place where the pack was sitting. He moved as he had done before, slowly but with determination, not attempting to conceal the sound of his arrival, telling the pack that he was coming. In a moment he saw eight wolves sitting in a semi-circle, their attention centred on him. The ritual began anew. Silverfeet stopped, wagged his tail, and bowed submission and friendship. He stood upright, tail still wagging, then advanced again and repeated his greeting. The pack waited for him.

In another moment they rose as a unit and advanced, surrounding him. But this pack was disposed to accept the newcomer. The pack leader was a bitch; she walked up to Silverfeet and extended her nose to him, smelling him. For a fraction of time the nine wolves stood poised in the moonglow. Of a sudden, the bitch pushed at Silverfeet, and this signalled the ritual attack on the stranger. He was mauled, snapped at, rolled over, but he offered no resistance. He knew by their actions, by the bloodless bites, that this pack, unlike the other, would accept him.

Suddenly the wolves lost interest in the testing of the newcomer. One by one they gave up and wandered off to lie or sit quietly under the trees. Silverfeet had come back to his own. Five minutes later the pack was at rest and Silverfeet lay with them, close to a young bitch of about his own age. In his eyes shone contentment. He curled up and sighed his happiness.

10

The bull moose stood like some prehistoric creature poised for battle. He stood seven feet tall at the shoulder, all four legs planted firmly, the snow reaching halfway to his knees. His long neck was outstretched, his spear-shaped ears were flattened to the sides of his head. From the bulbous nose spurted twin jets of snorted breath, forming clouds of vapour in the frigid air. He was big and dangerous, a giant of the forest with black, wiry mane erect over his humped shoulders and along his neck, ending just short of his antler bosses. He stood in a birch thicket, defiant, unmoving. He would not run from the pack.

Around him moved twelve wolves. They sought to stampede this monster, to break his nerve and make him run, and they feinted at him from all directions, darting in almost on top of him, turning as he swung for them with his front feet ready to slash and kill.

Silverfeet was in the forefront of the attack, running more

swiftly and more daringly than the others, twice snapping so close to the moose that the huge beast almost broke. He kept the pace brisk for perhaps five minutes; but the moose was stubborn, refusing to turn and run. Silverfeet ran in close one last time, jumping for the round belly of the moose. When the beast dodged and remained firm, the wolf backed away, stopped, and turned, moving silently to disappear into the birches. The others followed his lead.

Two years had passed since Silverfeet had killed Morgan and escaped into the northland, to be accepted by the pack that he now led. In that time he had grown to full stature, inheriting the size and power of his father. He had almost forgotten his deep hate. He had been taught anew by his companions' actions the immutable laws of the wolf hierarchy, and he had obeyed them. He had learned for the first time that pack wolves have evolved a class system — akin to that developed by man, but obeyed with greater frankness once a wolf has found his place within the social order of the pack. At first, Silverfeet, being the newcomer, was low in caste; he had accepted his place, until his size, strength and self-confidence exerted themselves and he climbed the social ladder, eventually attaining such respect from the others that his leadership was unquestioned.

He had mated with the young she by whose side he had stretched out the day the pack accepted him. The two had become companions immediately, but they did not mate until the following winter, when Silverfeet was two years old. And that spring, Silverfeet had fathered three pups.

The birth of his pups did more than anything else to expel the hate that now and then still rankled in his mind. He found in his fatherhood a bond between himself and the wilderness that was his heritage; he relearned the silent comradeship that was part of the life of the wolf pack. The pups had been born to his mate, and he had sired them; but they belonged as much to the pack as they did to their parents. Often one or another of the pack wolves fed the growing pups after a successful hunt;

never did they molest the youngsters, even when these, puppy-like, pestered a tired adult. At first Silverfeet kept a wary eye on his companions, but as he saw the affection that all the pack wolves showed for his young, he relaxed his vigilance, and later he adopted one more pack habit: he helped to look after some of the other pups as well as his own.

It had been a good year for the pack. Game was plentiful in the area of the rendezvous and all the pups thrived. Some of the young wolves of breeding age left the pack to seek mates of their own, so the pack did not grow in numbers beyond the point of efficiency. And this, too, was a law of the wild, a law which dictated that through death or migration each pack should multiply only to a point where there would be food for all.

Giving up on a moose that could not be made to run was normal wolf behaviour. The huge moose was a formidable foe, even for hunters as skilled as the wolves, and Silverfeet, after taking part in many hunts, knew that to stay and pester the angry, snorting giant was to court disaster. He had seen one of the pack killed by a moose during his first year of freedom and since that time he had always stayed clear of the fast hoofs. Today, though the pack was hungry, he swung away from the towering beast.

He led the wolves away from the bull, who was still snorting, blowing steam and occasionally scraping at the snow in slow-dying rage.

The pack was hungry; it had not eaten in four days. But all the wolves knew that they must run harder that day, and perhaps the next, before they could make a kill. And so they ran, spreading out through the birch forest, seeking fresh moose scent.

After half an hour one of the pack scented a fresh trail and swung onto it, and the rest followed. Silverfeet, as usual, ran a little harder and took the lead.

The quarry stood in a tangled patch of alders that bordered a beaver dam. It, too, was a bull moose, but older than the first. It threw up its head in alarm as the pack, now stretched in a single file, burst out of the birches and charged straight for it.

At first the moose stood its ground. It snorted and stamped and even made a lunge at one of the wolves, striking with one flashing foreleg. But it missed and threw itself off balance. At that instant Silverfeet nipped one of its hind legs. The moose swung quickly, its eyes showing white, fear replacing the anger. Silverfeet veered away and charged again, and three other wolves charged simultaneously. The moose broke. This was what the pack had sought.

As the great beast leaped away, long legs pumping like strange, jointed piston rods, Silverfeet spurted forward, leaped and bit the fugitive on the flank. He hung there for a moment, whirled through the air by his giant prey. Just as he felt himself slipping, he released his hold on the moose and kicked himself away to land lightly on his feet. Then he picked up his stride while the remainder of the pack worried the fugitive. One at a time, or in twos and threes, the wolves kept after the escaping moose, biting wherever they could, springing onto its rump, its neck, its withers, until the exhausted beast stopped, turned, and stood at bay.

The pack stopped too, forming a circle around the wounded moose, panting, the eager light of the hunt blazing in their yellow eyes. For a time they worried the moose, then they lay down and waited.

The moose stood slack, head hanging; then it dropped to its knees, attempting to rest. As soon as it was down the pack moved in, biting and snapping, forcing the great animal to its feet. The moose turned and ran. Again the wolves gave chase, repeating their previous tactics.

At last, Silverfeet, making a prodigious leap, landed on the back of the moose and sank his teeth into its neck. Other pack members tore at its flanks and rump. Their weight, and its own weakness, brought the moose crashing to the ground. Instantly the wolves were onto it, fangs sinking deep into flesh. Soon it was dead, and the pack settled to their feast. It might be days before they fed again; one or more of them might be killed by the great beasts that they hunted. But this was not now. It was enough for them that after fasting for four days, after three previous tries at downing a moose, they had succeeded. And they were content.

The warm sun of late June felt good on his back. Silverfeet lolled, taking his ease this afternoon after last night's hunt, his belly full of deer meat. He lay basking on a knoll near the den and there was pleasure in the eyes that settled, every now and then, on the five small pups that nursed from their mother's dugs. Around him some of the adult pack members reclined also, those who had not brought new life to the pack. It was a soft, balmy day of contentment for Silverfeet.

The sky was clear, and the air by its very softness instilled a sense of peace and well-being in the pack. A small bird sang, invisible in a bush. Somewhere, high in a tree, a red squirrel chattered. A stand of aspens rustled their heart-shaped leaves, and above this quiet medley sounded the huskier sighs of the pines. A few feet above ground-level, lacy wings buzzed softly as the many-hued dragonflies darted and swooped and circled in search of midges and mosquitoes.

Silverfeet rolled onto his chest and yawned. He grinned. And suddenly, lying there, he aimed his head at the sky and vented his pleasure in a series of musical calls. At once all the wolves joined him, some sitting, others lying, yet others standing. Their blended voices rose and fell in a spontaneous concert, prompted by a whim of pleasure. It was a pleasing melody. Half a mile away a buck deer, lowering his head in the act of grazing, raised it again, pricked up his ears for a moment and resumed nibbling at the grass, acknowledging the song of the wolves with a twitch of his white tail.

The throbbing voices of the wolves drifted over the forest and became lost. The song fell, was stilled. Silverfeet yawned again, and rolled onto his side, resting his head upon one big paw.

Once, years before, he had cried anguish. Today he cried wild.

EPILOGUE

Aided by field notes the first of which are dated 10 January, 1955, I recently completed a biological study of wolves and checked my data with those published by other investigators. I have also researched the history of man's feud with the species. What has emerged is an up-to-date biography of the wolf on which I am now drawing in order to write an epilogue to this book for those readers who may never have seen a wild wolf, or who may know little about the animal's biology.

I shall start by describing the wolf pack whose leader inspired me to write *Cry Wild* in 1969.

My acquaintance with these wolves began while I was doing field work in the wilderness of Ontario, working from a small headquarters cabin which I built in a relatively open section of the forest. On an afternoon in autumn, soon after I had finished the construction, I returned from an exploratory canoe trip to find that, in my absence, wolves had visited my dwelling and had urinated against it, their actions telling me that they considered the land occupied by the cabin to be a part of their territory.

By this time I had been observing wolves for more than twenty years, so I was neither surprised nor intimidated by the pack's behaviour. On the contrary! By marking my dwelling as they did, they were also telling me that they would return on a regular basis, for when these animals concentrate their urine on one particular object in such a definite way, they are deliberately setting up a scent station, a place that will be visited and wetted whenever the pack finds itself in its vicinity.

Every pack regularly maintains many such stations within the boundaries of its territory, the intent being to advertise the fact that the section of forest in which the wolves live is occupied and, therefore, out of bounds to other packs; neighbouring wolves are, however, frequently tolerated provided that these do not seek to occupy the range permanently. Should such an event occur, the incumbent wolves will attack the intruders during a series of skirmishes that end in victory for the strongest pack, although such altercations are rare: wolves are imbued with a strong, inherent sense of territoriality that causes trespassers to respect the rights of their neighbours and to feel uneasy whenever they cross marked boundaries.

Like all wild hunters, however, wolves tolerate within their range, but with one exception, predators that belong to different species, such as mountain lions, bears, wolverines, lynxes and others. With these they co-exist in what may be termed a state of armed neutrality, each kind of animal respecting the others, provided that competition for meat does not become severe during times when prey populations go into decline in response to overcrowding and depletion of their food resources. Such die-offs occur from time to time amongst all wild species. When prey numbers remain stable, wolves will rarely attack other predators, even when some of these share the pack's kills after its members have taken their fill and left the remains. The exception noted earlier is the coyote (*Canis latrans*), a small, jackal-like wolf found in North and Central America that grey wolves view as a competitor and therefore kill whenever they have an opportunity to do so, although the dead coyotes are rarely eaten by their large relatives. Nevertheless, because coyotes are artful dodgers, a number of them manage to survive in wolf country.

In Canada, the United States and Mexico, for reasons that will be noted later, man is never personally molested by wolves. The opposite holds true, for while our species continues to persecute it, the animal usually avoids us. As I have proved on many occasions, wolves will come to accept man and even show considerable interest in him, once they are satisfied that he means them no harm. Thus it was that when I was made to realise that I had built my cabin in the territory of a pack, I went out of my way to show that I was both harmless and friendly, in this way hoping that I would be given an opportunity to study the wolves on a long-term basis. To demonstrate good will, I began putting out scraps of meat, bones, and commercial dogfood, which I always placed on a bare, flat rock within sight of the east window of my small dwelling.

At first the wolves came only at night, eating the food and thereafter disappearing into the forest without my immediate awareness, but leaving behind their tracks and urine stains for me to find the next morning. Then, by mid-winter, the seven wolves that made up the pack at that time began to appear soon after dawn, their arrival heralded by the leader, or Alpha male, who approached alone and with great caution, stopping often to scan my building, sniff the air, and listen for alien sounds. When satisfied that all was well, the big wolf advanced and started to eat and soon afterwards his mate, the Alpha female, came to join him. While the two were feeding, the other wolves hovered nearby, hoping to be allowed to eat a mouthful or two. But the leaders rarely gave them an opportunity to do so.

The first time that I noticed the lead wolf's daytime arrival, I stood back from the window so that my movements would not be detected and watched through field glasses; the distance between us was about one hundred yards. The Alpha was a handsome animal of slaty-grey colour above, but lighter below, his front legs being almost white. The early sun spilled a shaft over his feet, giving them a silver sheen; and it was this momentary illusion that was later to cause me to name the main protagonist of this book.

As I watched the wolf, his mystical, amber-coloured eyes kept rising from his meal in order to inspect my dwelling, momentary stares that, I knew, absorbed every single detail that lay within the perimeters of his vision. Typical of his kind, his senses were ever on the alert; and when his mate emerged from the forest and loped towards him, followed by the rest of the pack, the way that his ears swivelled backwards, then returned to their normal, forward position made it clear that he had instantly recognised them by the highly individualistic ways in which each moved, the sounds and rhythms of their gaits being permanently recorded in his memory together with their scent and, indeed, all their personal mannerisms. Similarly, his mate and subordinates were just as intimate with the characteristics and habits of their leader as well as with those of their companions, for this, too, is typical of all wolves.

When the entire pack was assembled before me, it became evident by the way in which the grey exacted obedience from his subordinates that his rule was absolute. Yet he was no despot, being himself governed by the disciplines imposed on all wolves everywhere by thousands of years of natural order. Because of this, he was aware that the well-being, the very survival of the pack, was his responsibility; so, as Alpha wolves have done since the dawn of creation, he led by example and he merited the respect and affection of all his subordinates. When he had to punish, as I was later to see him do on a number of occasions, he did so swiftly, but with discretion; then, just as quickly, he immediately offered forgiveness and reassurance. When I had seen him initially and despite the fact that he was then on his own, I had needed but a glance to know that he was a leader. He reflected his status by the way that he carried himself, his entire being denoting dignity and confidence and great intelligence. And the very fact that he came alone, while his subordinates waited within the safety of the trees, showed that he was conscious of his responsibilities. He knew that there was need for caution in any location where the scent of man was strong and fresh, so he deliberately exposed himself to possible risks, approaching carefully and reconnoitring fully until he was satisfied that no danger lurked nearby; then he relaxed, and his change of stance and movement told his companions that they could also approach.

In the past I had seen many similar examples of risk taking by a wolf leader, so I knew that the grey's behaviour was usual, but as I watched him, it occurred to me that those of us who know the wolf and have deep empathy with him often discover to our astonishment that he possesses all of our best attributes and none of our weaknesses. Furthermore, I thought, judging by those humans who still maintain close family unity, wolf hierarchy is not very different from that which probably governed early hominids, when related individuals lived and hunted together as a family under the control and direction of responsible male and female leaders.

Later, watching the two Alphas prevent their subordinates from eating any of the food that I had put out, it would have been easy to believe that they were being selfish. In fact, such behaviour is prompted by need. Lead wolves are the guardians of the pack and the responsibilities of their stewardship are such that they must expend a great deal more energy than their subordinates, while at the same time they are subject to higher levels of stress. For these reasons, they must remain strong for the good of all. They therefore exercise their authority and eat first, although when food is available in adequate amounts, subordinates are usually allowed to feed off the kill in the company of their leaders after the latter have partially satisfied their hunger. Because the amount of food that I was in the habit of putting out was hardly enough to satisfy one wolf, let alone seven, the Alphas kept it for themselves. In fact, what I offered them was really little more than a titbit, a few mouthfuls for each Alpha that they came to collect, in all probability, after they had already hunted and eaten between ten and twenty pounds of meat each, the amount depending upon how much time had elapsed since the pack had taken a deer or moose. From earlier surveys of the region, I knew that there were more than enough prey animals living in it to sustain the pack, all of the members of which were in excellent condition when I first saw them and were to remain so during the course of the entire winter.

As matters turned out, my acquaintance with this pack lasted almost five years, until I had to leave the area to undertake new field work. During that time, I became so well accepted by the wolves that I was able to watch them openly, sometimes from distances of twenty yards or less. In due course I named the leader Lobo and in my notes I referred to the family as the Lobo Pack, to distinguish it from a second group of wolves that occupied a territory some miles to the east of my location, which I was also able to observe during the same period.

Thus, for fifty-seven months, I monitored the life of the Lobo

Pack, sharing with the wolves some times of tragedy and many moments of triumph, especially during and after the mating seasons, when on three occasions I was privileged to watch the courtship of the two leaders and, later, to observe for days at a time the ways in which the wolves cared for and educated their cubs.

*   *   *

Fossil evidence suggests that a primitive carnivore that has been given the name of *Tomarctos* emerged during the Upper Miocene Period, some twenty-five million years ago. This creature, according to those who research the antecedents of prehistoric animals, gave rise to the *Canidae*, or dog family, to which have been assigned some 34 species, including the grey wolf (*Canis lupus*), the coyote, the foxes, and such exotic animals as the raccoon-like dog of east Asia; the Culpeo of Bolivia, Chile, and Tierra del Fuego, and the maned wolf of Bolivia, Paraguay and Argentina.

The grey wolf, although it has been divided into some thirty sub-species around the world, is the animal that I have written about in this book. Some biologists may become upset by the fact that I insist on calling a wolf a *wolf*, but I am sticking to my guns because I do not share the scientific mania for naming sub-species of animals unless the differences encountered are readily observable. In the case of the wolf, it is impossible to detect the different sub-species by sight and, whatever anatomical variations are to be noted, these are only revealed through necropsy, which is the biologist's term for autopsy. Certainly, there are observable differences in the colour and size of wolves, but these are not necessarily restricted to particular regions. White wolves are common in the far north, but, although rarer, they are also encountered in more southern areas. Black wolves are never plentiful, but they are not *rare*, and may be encountered in almost all ranges. Grey is the shade most frequently used to describe the coats of wolves, but this designation is far too specific, for pure greys are uncommon.

Most wolves show an admixture of shades and colours besides grey, including rufous bands and irregular markings of black, cream, fawn, and brown among which areas of white are conspicuous, particularly on legs and undersides. Seen from a distance, however, and especially against the light or in the penumbra of the forest, many wolves do *look* grey.

In the matter of weight, the variations are great in all regions. In more southerly parts, male wolves may weigh between 80 pounds and, in extreme cases, 110 pounds. Females in all areas are about 20 per cent lighter and smaller. In the extreme north, males will weigh between 100 pounds and, again in extreme cases, 160 pounds. On the other hand, it is by no means uncommon to find small wolves in the north and large ones in the south.

However these things may be, and before mankind began to overpopulate the world, *Canis lupus* lived right around the northern hemisphere, the only barriers to its southerly distribution being deserts and jungles, in both of which habitats the wolf cannot survive. In North America, wolves were found from the high Arctic all the way south to the edges of the deserts and tropical areas of Mexico. Across the Atlantic, they lived in Britain, all over Europe, in Asia, and in suitable territories of north-west Africa, but by the sixteenth century, for example, wolves had become extinct in England. In Ireland, the animals hung on until the late seventeenth century, when the last of them were killed. In 1743 wolves also became extinct in Scotland.

At the turn of the nineteenth century, wolves were still relatively common in most of Europe and Asia except for a corridor of extinction that began in southern France, at the Spanish border, and travelled north-eastwards through parts of Belgium, Holland and Germany. By 1973, the numbers of wolves in Europe and Russia had dropped dramatically and today, the animals are either extinct or endangered throughout most of their historical ranges.

In North America, wolves have been virtually wiped out in 47 of the 48 states that lie south of the Canadian border, the exception being Minnesota, where about 1,200 wolves still exist and are more or less protected by law because the US federal government has placed them on the threatened species list. In Alaska, which still has a relatively viable population of wolves, the animals are not protected by federal law. As a result, under pressure from sport hunters who want to kill more moose, caribou and other so-called big game animals, the state government has in recent years been killing wolves by shooting them from aircraft, by trapping, and by poisoning.

Canada has a good population of wolves within its northern wilderness areas, but several provincial governments (and especially British Columbia) have been killing them by various means, once again responding to pressure from sport hunters.

Nevertheless, because more and more people have begun to understand the importance of wolves within the scheme of nature, numerous conservation groups in North America are now actively campaigning for the preservation of the species; and although it may be too early at this time to express confidence, it is likely that wolves will continue to exist in Canada, Alaska and Minnesota.

The first real attempt to study wolves did not begin until 1940, when Dr Adolph Murie, an internationally respected American biologist, initiated a field research programme in Alaska. Since then, literally hundreds of scientists have studied the behaviour and ecology of the animals. As a result, the bad press received by the wolf for centuries is slowly being replaced by favourable publicity, but despite the fact that more is known about wolves today than at any other time in history, those of us who have studied the animal over long periods realise that there is much yet to learn about its life. Indeed, whenever I come into contact with wolves, they teach me something new about themselves, as Lobo and his pack did so frequently during the years of our acquaintance.

* * *

One of the most haunting sounds to be heard in the wilderness is the call of the wolf, a deep, long-drawn and magnificently primordial song that is voiced for a variety of reasons, some of which are not yet fully understood. More recently, it has been suggested that wolves howl so as to confuse a neighbouring pack that might have hostile intentions, the purported reason for this theory being that when a pack calls in unison, the varying pitch of their voices may deceive a listener into believing that the number of wolves in the group is greater than it really is. This argument also contends that when pups are on their own in a rendezvous, they deepen their voices when they sing so as to imply that adults are present with them, in this way deceiving any other wolves that might be tempted to seek them out and kill them. I do not subscribe to such opinions. They imply that wolves are almost always at war with each other, which they are not. They also fail to take into account that pups would be much safer from a supposed attack if they did not advertise their presence by howling!

Why, then, *do* wolves sing? They do so when they are happy; they do so when they are sad; they sing together much as humans do when we are clustered around a piano; they sing before a hunt, no doubt because they are excited at the prospect; they call to each other so as to keep in touch, to *communicate*; lone wolves howl to attract a mate; they call so as to tell others of their kind that their territory is already occupied, thus reinforcing the messages left at their scent stations and ensuring peaceful co-existence with their neighbours. But most of all, I believe wolves sing because they enjoy it!

When the breeding season begins to stir their hormones, wolves become excited and sing a great deal, remaining restless until the Alpha pair have mated, although there are occasions when the male leader shows no interest in his mate, who is then likely to become temporarily paired with the Beta male. Such behaviour is not usual. That it occurs at all, and *why* it does, are questions yet to be answered. Interestingly, however, the pups fathered by the Beta male are cared for by the Alpha pair in exactly the same way that they would be if the male leader had actually sired them.

Breeding times vary, in the far north being common during the last week of March and the first week of April (sometimes as late as early May) and in more southerly regions during the third week of February, the timing intended to produce young in early spring, when the weather has moderated.

Unlike domestic dog females, which have two periods of oestrus annually, wolf females breed only once a year, principally because life in the wild is too harsh to support two litters every twelve months, but also because this is one way in which nature balances wolf populations.

Gestation takes about 63 days, the same as for domestic dogs, and, therefore, a wolf that has mated during the third week of February will give birth to from two to as many as fourteen cubs during the last week of April or the first week of May. An average litter probably consists of six or seven pups during normal times. Cub mortality rates, however, are high; perhaps only two out of a litter of six or seven pups will survive to accompany the pack during the next winter. Even so, when it is considered that wolves are hosts to one-hundred-and-thirty-four different kinds of viruses and parasites, the survival rate could almost be regarded as high, and it certainly testifies to the remarkable endurance of the species. Surprisingly, however, the most dreaded of all diseases, rabies, is not a serious killer of wolves and coyotes, both of which appear to have developed strong resistance to the virus, this information having been recently documented by American scientists.

Wolf cubs come into the world fully furred, their coats being either a slaty blue or a dark brown colour. Weighing about one pound, their legs are not fully developed at birth; they are blind, and their hearing is not acute during the first days of life. But the pups develop rapidly, averaging a weight gain of about two pounds a week. Some time between the tenth and twelfth days, their eyes open, the pupils being blue and remaining so until the cubs are about two months old, when, gradually, beginning in the centre of each pupil and working outwards, the blue is replaced by the amber-yellow colour so characteristic of all wolves. By now the cubs begin to howl and growl in response to hunger or sibling rivalry, for already each is seeking to dominate the other, preparing themselves in this way for a place within the hierarchy of the pack and, perhaps two or three years later, for the day when they may leave the family in order to form their own social group.

Wolf puppies are born in a den that may be dug by their mother and other members of the pack, or may be located in a cave, or even within a suitable cavity among a jumble of rocks. Whenever possible, wolves prefer to site their dens on a height of land, ideally in reasonably open country from where they have a good view of their surroundings. If the ground is suitable, the mother digs a tunnel that may be twenty to thirty feet long before it ends in an oval chamber, the centre of which has been scooped out to a depth of four or five inches. On the bare earth of this basin-like depression, the cubs emerge one at a time. As each is born, the mother bites through its umbilical cord – although this may break by itself – and then licks the cub dry. Afterwards she uses her nose to push it against her stomach so that the newborn can begin to nurse on one of her eight teats.

When the cubs are born, all the wolves exhibit great excitement. There is much socialising between individuals, tail-wagging, playing, and eager whining at the den entrance as last year's young and the adults sniff and listen for the cries of the puppies. At this stage, only the mother cares for them, not even the father being allowed into the den for the next ten days or so, despite the fact that he conscientiously brings food to the mother, carrying meat in his mouth, or having swallowed it first, regurgitating it at the tunnel entrance.

At first, cubs look more like little bears than wolves. They are stubby in the body, their ears flop forward, their muzzles are short and their tails skinny. But when they are about three weeks old and begin to emerge from the den, they are starting to acquire a lupine appearance. Now, although they will continue nursing from their mother until they are between 45 and 50 days old, they also begin to eat meat, at first doing little more than chewing feebly with teeth that are mere pinpoints, but nevertheless absorbing juices and small bits of flesh. By the time another week has passed, their teeth may measure three-eighths of an inch and they can eat more solid food. At this time they play with each other, explore the immediate environs of the den and pester the adults, biting and scrambling over them and sometimes becoming thorough-going nuisances with almost complete immunity, for they are rather spoiled at this stage of their lives.

After they have been weaned and have been consuming only meat for two or three weeks, the pups probably weigh about fourteen pounds. They are still quite pampered, but they are sometimes disciplined mildly by the parents, or by an aunt or elder female sibling.

Despite the fact that wolves dote on their young and always look forward to their arrival each spring, a form of birth control is practised by the species. If a pack survives the winter with its numbers undiminished, only the Alpha female will mate and smaller litters appear to be the rule. Other females in the pack come into oestrus, but the presence of the Alpha pair usually inhibits the sexual drives of all subordinate wolves. If, nevertheless, a female solicits a male, the two leaders punish her, a task in which they are often assisted by the males, all of which, despite the fact that their own sexual urges may be aroused, subdue their desires in favour of supporting their leaders.

When pack numbers have been reduced during the preceding winter by accidents, disease, or human control measures, or if prey animal numbers have radically increased, thus offering abundant food, it is not uncommon, under such circumstances, fot the Beta female of a pack to mate with the Beta male, in this way increasing the pack numbers to a degree compatible with the food resources.

During times when a pack's population is in balance with prey numbers and a subordinate female shows signs of being a serious breeding competitor, the Alpha pair harass her to such an extent that she will be forced to leave the pack. Should such an ousted female happen to meet a lone male from another pack at this time, the two will be likely to mate and thus form their own family unit in an adjacent territory, if this is available; or, migrating, they will search for an unoccupied range in which to settle. If the ousted wolf does not encounter a suitor, she will stay in touch with her pack by means of sound and scent, keeping out of sight but following the group and even sharing their kills when the latter have left the scene. When the new pups are born, however, the ostracised bitch will rejoin her pack and will be made welcome, in all probability appointing herself guardian of the pups once these have been weaned and in this way serving a useful function as relief for the mother, while at the same time experiencing the fulfilment of motherhood without actually carrying and delivering the pups.

By their first autumn, wolf cubs are almost as large as the adults and are fully capable of participating in the hunt, the techniques of which they have learned by observing their parents, elder siblings, or aunts and uncles during a process of learning that begins soon after they are old enough to leave their summer nursery, some time during August. Such nurseries, referred to by biologists as *rendezvous*, are locations some distance from the birth den. The cubs are moved there soon after they are weaned. An ideal rendezvous will offer sufficient natural cover in which the young wolves can hide if danger threatens in the absence of the pack, but it will also have open areas where the cubs can romp and dig and practise their craft by hunting mice and voles. When they are moved to the rendezvous by the mother, who is sometimes helped by the Beta female, they are carried by mouth, usually being grasped by the middle of the body; but sometimes they may be carried by the hindquarters, or even by the head.

*   *   *

It has been said that wolves are cunning hunters who have developed a variety of tactics for the ambush of their prey, much as lions are known to do in Africa. This is not so. Wolves are runners. They chase large prey animals and are able to continue a pursuit for long distances, running tirelessly at about ten miles an hour, although during chases they may attain speeds of 25 or 30 miles an hour. Here, too, some writers have greatly exaggerated the wolf's top speed, claiming that it can go as fast as 40 miles an hour, a rate that would exceed that of its prey. The truth is that prey animals are always faster than their predators: if they were not, the probability is that they would soon become extinct, in which case the hunters would also die off. Some predators (such as a cheetah), can attain high rates of speed over a short chase, others, like the wolf, are long-distance runners that have the stamina to tire their target animal; but it should be noted that a pack may chase between eight and thirteen different prey animals before they manage to kill one.

Occasionally, because of terrain, a wolf pack will split up, some going to the right of a natural barrier, the others to the left. If they are fortunate, it may happen that one half of the pack will find itself in front of the prey because of the detour, and thus be in a position to make a quick kill. But this is the exception rather than the rule and it occurs by accident rather than by design. A lone wolf, however, engaged in hunting small prey, such as hares, grouse and the like, *will* resort to stealth, stalking the quarry and often enough lying in ambush, prone to the ground and unmoving, if the prey animal is travelling towards it.

When hunting adult moose, wolves must attack on the run, for these large members of the deer family are too powerful and dangerous to be seized if they stand at bay, which they often do. In such cases, the wolves will surround the animal and make periodic bluff charges at it. If, after about twenty minutes, the moose refuses to be panicked, the pack will move on, searching for an individual that can be made to run. When that occurs, and the wolves can eventually attack, they aim for the rump or flanks in order to cause the moose to stumble and fall, whereupon it is soon killed. But sometimes a wolf may only manage to grasp a shoulder, or the neck, dangerous holds because the quarry may smash its attacker against a tree and probably kill it.

An adult moose at bay is a formidable adversary. Using either of its front feet as weapons, it can "stab-kick" a wolf and kill it with one slash of the pointed hoof. If the moose is thus engaged and another wolf seeks to attack it from the rear, the big deer will lash out with a back hoof, much as a horse will do. If such a blow connects, it may well kill the attacker, or at least injure it so severely that it may die later, although there are records of wolves feeding an injured companion until it was well enough to resume hunting with the pack.

Whether its native range happens to be in North America or elsewhere in the world, *Canis lupus* is undoubtedly the most social and adaptable of all mammals, man excepted; and the ways in which he interacts with his fellows and governs his affairs are truly remarkable; so much so, in fact, that it seems to me that once the wolf is better understood, he will offer our species some much-needed lessons in social deportment and will almost certainly teach us how to manage our environment in ecologically-sound ways; this despite the fact that humans have for centuries hated, feared and relentlessly persecuted the wolf. Yet, available evidence tells us that primitive people have always held the wolf in high esteem, while prehistoric man, seeing the advantages of an alliance with such an efficient hunter, tamed him and used him in the chase, many of today's breeds of dogs stemming from that ancient liaison.

The feud between man and wolf undoubtedly began in Europe during historical times, when burgeoning human populations caused more and more forested land to be cleared for agriculture. As the wilderness shrank and natural prey animals declined drastically, wolves started to kill domestic stock. At about this time, rabies, which, as noted, is not a major problem in the wild, reached epidemic proportions when it encountered the many vagrant domestic dogs that in those times were free to roam from community to community. As the epidemic spread, near starving wolves that had entered villages in search of prey, came into contact with rabid dogs and became infected, for no wolf is completely immune to the sickness. People were bitten by rabid animals and were condemned to a dreadful death – this was long before Pasteur developed the rabies vaccine – and large, wolf-dog hybrids marauded singly and in packs, attacking humans and animals alike. In consequence, hatred for the wolf became so deeply rooted in the human psyche that it survives unabated today in many people, despite the fact that it has been definitely established that healthy wolves do not attack humans.

Predators become programmed on their prey in the nursery, where they learn the taste and scent of those animals that their parents bring home for them. As adults, they naturally seek out the prey that they have been accustomed to eating, although they will kill other wild animals and domestic stock in the absence of preferred prey species. But man, because he walks upright and thus does not move like all other mammals, and because he carries with him many of the scents of his civilised world (which are mostly unnatural), is not looked upon as prey. Then, too, because wolves are extremely intelligent, they quickly learn – and remember – to associate the scent of man with that of his traps, guns, and poisons. So they avoid him and fear him.

When I first came into contact with wild wolves, they intimidated me from a distance, as I have already noted. But my second, and much closer encounter was even more frightening, for a pack of eight wolves surrounded me and kept circling me while howl-barking in a manner that I immediately interpreted as threatening. Forming a ring that was about forty feet in diameter, the pack continued to make a fuss until, fearful of an attack, I plucked up enough nerve to seek escape, whereupon the circle parted and I was allowed to leave. Returning to the scene later, armed with a gun, it was to find that the wolves had gone; but they had left behind the remains of a deer that they had killed. I had actually interrupted them while they were eating and they had conspired to bluff me to very good effect. I have not feared wolves since that day.

I have to date observed 351 wolves belonging to 39 packs. At no time have I ever been in any danger, despite the fact that I have slept under the stars in the middle of wolf territory and have frequently awakened in the morning to discover from tracks and urine marks that a pack had investigated me during the night, sometimes coming to within a few feet of my slumbering form.

Once, in 1967, I was awakened at dawn by what I at first thought to be rain drumming on the canvas that I had spread over my sleeping bag to ward off the dampness. But when I raised my head, I saw Lobo, who had just urinated on the foot of my bed and was even then lowering a back leg, his actions watched with interest by the other wolves, who were grouped together at a place some ten feet away. On noticing that I had wakened, Lobo backed away a short distance, scratched the ground with both hind feet, turned, gave me a sideways look, and then led his pack into the forest.

As I write this, my wife, Sharon, and I are caring for two yearling wolves that we rescued from death in the Yukon Territory in the spring of 1984, when they were only 23 days old. We have named the male Tundra; he is black, with a white star on his chest. His sister's name is Taiga and she is a "grey" wolf, which is to say that her coat has a peppering of grey and black and a series of markings that vary from rufous, to brown, fawn, and white. Daily we enter the one-and-a-half-acre enclosure in which our friends live, feed them raw meat by hand and romp with them. Tundra weighs more than 80 pounds and his sister 70 pounds. Like all wolves, they are exceptionally powerful, but they are also gentle when they close their jaws on our hands or arms by way of giving us a lupine greeting. Our relationship is one of mutual love, which is something that wolves give freely.

In an undisturbed environment, wolves are finely tuned to the wilderness and are completely free of the sins that have been attributed to them. They are, of course, hunters, but they kill only out of need when opportunity presents itself; and they must often go hungry for days at a time. They are not, as legend has it, wanton, cruel or greedy. In fact, I know from personal experience that wolves actually eat less than a domestic dog of equivalent size. And when full, nothing will induce them to eat, not even if they are offered the most tempting morsels.

As I have noted in all the wolves I have studied, and especially in the Lobo Pack and in Tundra and Taiga, wolves are generally peaceful among themselves. Indeed, to date our two wolves have never had a fight! Nevertheless, occasional territorial disputes or status fights do occur and may lead to the death of an individual wolf. But such hostilities are few and similar to those that occur among all species of animals, none of which – with the exception of humans – make war on each other.